PUFFIN CANADA

LAST CHANCE BAY

ANNE LAUREL CARTER is the author of the Our Canadian Girl: Elizabeth series, as well as *Under a Prairie Sky*, *The Girl on Evangeline Beach*, *Tall in the Saddle*, and *From Poppa*. She has won the Mr. Christie's Book Award, the Vicky Metcalf Award for short stories, and the Thistledown Young Adult Short Story Competition. She lives in Toronto.

Also by Anne Laurel Carter

Our Canadian Girl: Elizabeth
Bless This House
To Pirate Island
A Hornbook Christmas
Wide as Wings

The F Team

My Home Bay

Circus Play

No Missing Parts

Under a Prairie Sky

In the Clear

The Girl on Evangeline Beach

Tall in the Saddle

From Poppa

The Shepherd's Granddaughter

Out of the Deeps

LAST CHANCE BAY

ANNE LAUREL CARTER

PUFFIN
CANADA

PUFFIN CANADA

Published by the Penguin Group

Penguin Group (Canada), 90 Eglinton Avenue East, Suite 700,
Toronto, Ontario, Canada M4P 2Y3 (a division of Pearson Canada Inc.)

Penguin Group (USA) Inc., 375 Hudson Street, New York, New York 10014, U.S.A.
Penguin Books Ltd, 80 Strand, London WC2R 0RL, England
Penguin Ireland, 25 St Stephen's Green, Dublin 2, Ireland
(a division of Penguin Books Ltd)
Penguin Group (Australia), 250 Camberwell Road, Camberwell,
Victoria 3124, Australia (a division of Pearson Australia Group Pty Ltd)
Penguin Books India Pvt Ltd, 11 Community Centre, Panchsheel Park,
New Delhi – 110 017, India
Penguin Group (NZ), 67 Apollo Drive, Rosedale, North Shore 0632,
New Zealand (a division of Pearson New Zealand Ltd)
Penguin Books (South Africa) (Pty) Ltd, 24 Sturdee Avenue, Rosebank,
Johannesburg 2196, South Africa

Penguin Books Ltd, Registered Offices: 80 Strand, London WC2R 0RL, England

First published in Penguin Canada paperback by Penguin Group (Canada),
a division of Pearson Canada Inc., 2004
Published in this edition, 2009

1 2 3 4 5 6 7 8 9 10 (OPM)

Lines quoted on page 138 are from "Dulce Et Decorum Est" by Wilfred Owen.

Manufactured in the U.S.A.

Library and Archives Canada Cataloguing in Publication data available
upon request to the publisher.

ISBN: 978-0-14-316949-9

To Savino "Hinson" Calabrese,
the Cape Breton Miners' Museum,
and miners' families everywhere

LAST CHANCE BAY

CHAPTER 1

For the longest time, right up until my fourteenth birthday, I wanted to wake up as a boy. It's not that I wanted big muscles or facial hair, and for sure I didn't want to beat the bejesus out of someone every lunch hour. I wanted to fly a plane—fly it right off Cape Breton Island. Here in Last Chance Bay, you had to be a boy to get off the ground.

I'd finished my Latin and was indulging in my favourite daydream, while Miss MacKinnon glided between the rows of desks. *Veni, vidi, vici.* The words of Caesar, "I came, I saw, I conquered," lulled me into a dreamy state. The famous pilot

Amelia Earhart wasn't dead but alive and coming to meet me. Half in focus, I could see the young ones bobbing in the front row, struggling with Latin verbs. The middle rows were writing the names of cities and the occupied countries on their maps of Europe. Here, in the back rows, right beside me …

Jumping Judas, I should never have looked. Jason MacDonald was doing a little housecleaning in his nose. Why didn't he lie about his age and enlist in the war? Or stay outside with his mangy dog? What a beam head! Last week Miss MacKinnon confided to us that Providence—that was her fancy word for God—had sent her to our one-room schoolhouse. She said she loved all forty-three of us … but I know she was lying about Jason.

I should never have agreed to sit here. One day after school last November, Miss MacKinnon had kept me behind to ask "a favour." Private-like.

"You're my best student, Meg. I'd like you to sit between Maurice"—we called him Frenchie—"and Jason. You'll be a good influence on the back row."

Sit with the boys? It was bad enough living with my bratty brother, Will. In terms of heroes, Miss

MacKinnon was right up there with Amelia Earhart, but this was a lot to ask. I had to think it over.

The girls couldn't believe it when I told them at recess.

"Why'd she ask you?" Jane Watson asked enviously.

What a typical no-brainer from that girl! My mother said I suffered from Jane Watson envy. NOT true. I didn't want to be like her, although it bugged me whenever the boys, especially my older cousin Caleb, wanted to walk her home. It bugged me too that the girls treated her like our leader when she didn't have an original thought or brave bone in her body.

"You'll be pregnant by summer," Bozana Zawada said. "They leave something on the seats."

I liked Bozana. She had lots of original thoughts and wasn't afraid to say them. Bozana's family was Polish, and if I envied anyone, it was Bozana. Her mother taught piano lessons. When you walked by Bozana's house, you didn't hear arguments but music that made you stop and dream.

You'd think Last Chance Bay was a beautiful place for all the people it attracted. We were mostly Scottish, but also Polish, Italian, French,

English, and Irish. We used to have Germans, the Kraus family, only we sent them to a detention camp after the war broke out. My dad said that was a mean, senseless thing to do. The only rebellious thing Wilhelm Kraus had ever done was build a little garden two miles under the earth so the miners could smell a few geraniums. Wilhelm and his wife had lived in Last Chance Bay for thirty years, and their kids didn't speak a word of German. They were as Canadian as a MacDonald or a Christie.

"What are we afraid of?" my dad argued. "Do we think Willie Kraus is going to blow up his own home?"

But then a German U-boat sank the ferry from Sydney to Newfoundland. Everybody was terrified of anybody with a German name. Sydney wasn't across the ocean in Europe. It was the next town, only a tramcar ride away. Mom made Dad promise to keep his opinions around our kitchen table.

Anyway, no matter what country our ancestors came from, ever since we were little girls in the front row, we believed that sitting in the back row would get us pregnant. That's because every older girl who sat there soon dropped out of school to have a baby, followed by a wedding. My mother told me that was not the right order to do things, but I wasn't worried. I had no intention of doing either.

I wasn't going to marry a boy in Last Chance Bay. It made no difference where their grandparents were from: they were all headed straight for the coal mine. Even my wonderful cousin Caleb. There was only one thing in life worthy of my attention: getting up in a plane.

My latest plan was to dress up as a boy and join the Royal Canadian Air Force. Or maybe I'd get myself to England the way Horace Feldman did a few years ago, by stowing away on a transatlantic bomber.

Miss MacKinnon was moving to the front of the room. It was time to stop daydreaming.

"Get out your printing books," she said quietly. "Ten lines of *Terra Firma*. That's Latin for 'the ground beneath us.' If you were Odysseus at sea, that's what you'd be looking for."

There was a rustle of papers. Bobbing heads became waves on the Mediterranean casting out lines for land. Miss MacKinnon's brown hair shone with golden streaks and she carried her pencil like an enchanted sword. It was really thanks to her that I felt hope that my dreams would come true. She agreed I needed to get out of Last Chance Bay. But she had a different plan for me. I'd write the provincial exams in two years and go to school in Boston States. Talk about *terra firma*. Where did she think we'd get the money for me to go to America? Who was going to convince my mother that I needed it?

I indulged in another daydream. Amelia Earhart, the famous aviatrix who had disappeared while flying across the Pacific in 1937, was miraculously rescued after living on a tropical island for seven years. When she found out there was a war going on, she offered to fly to England to train new pilots. A storm forced her to land in a bog near our mine. I found her and she invited me up in her plane. I was flying with Amelia over Last Chance Bay. The Atlantic Ocean was below me, waves bobbing—

A sound brought me back to reality. Something outside. Miss MacKinnon's voice stopped, and we all listened to the sound of running footsteps coming closer. Outside on the gravel road, someone was running to the school. We turned around to see the door thrown open.

It was Caleb, panting and out of breath. What was Caleb doing here? After his dad broke his leg under the coal car in February, Caleb had quit school to work in the mine.

Caleb scanned the faces in the room. He didn't stop at his own brothers and sisters. He paused at Will, then his eyes found mine.

"Meg. It's your dad. There's been—"

The scream of a siren exploded around us, the siren that said there was an accident at the mine.

I stopped thinking. I had only one wish now. Everyone stared at Miss MacKinnon. Her face went tight. The light in her hair went out.

"Class dismissed."

Chairs scraped. Feet pounded. The other kids made way for Will and me. At times like this, it was good to have a brother. I grabbed his hand. On wings of fear Will and I flew down the dirt road toward the mine with the same thought, one prayer rising from the dust.

Let Dad be okay.

CHAPTER 2

There'd been a cave-in. Uncle Art and Caleb stood with us while we waited for a rescue team to dig out the tunnel in which Dad was trapped two miles below the surface of the earth. The whole town stood behind us. Mom was quiet. Uncle Art, smelling faintly of whiskey, stood beside her. The miners stood with their families, talking. At first, I couldn't hear what they were saying, but as the minutes ticked by, I overheard snippets of conversation.

"Hey, Vince! Remember the day years ago when you came up with your hand hanging off by a tendon?"

"Mining's dangerous. Don't nobody ever tell you different."

I stared at Vince Calabrese, remembering the day he lost his hand. I remembered, too, how the war made us suspect all Italians of being enemies. How the town that once gathered food and money for the Calabrese family suddenly turned against him. Vince Calabrese and some other Italians had been sent to a detention camp just as Wilhelm Kraus had. But the Italians didn't blow up any Canadian ferries. Dad and some other miners spoke up for Mr. Calabrese and the Italians at the union meeting, and they were back at work nine months later.

"The company cares more about lumps of coal than our lives."

"If we were smart, we'd leave these godforsaken pits and this island."

"I hear Jack MacIsaac is living the high life in Boston States."

"There's no mines waiting to kill you in Boston States."

"Not unless you light a stick of dynamite in the middle of the city."

They all laughed. If you were smart enough to land a job in Boston States, you wouldn't go disturbing the earth's foundations any more. Humans weren't meant to be underground. The earth's foundations didn't like being disturbed. Any fool knew that.

Every now and then I'd hear a hymn, sometimes in Italian, sometimes in Polish or Gaelic. Will and I stared at the mouth of the mine shaft, unable to look anyone in the eye. Someone commented that we looked like twins. We both had a small face fringed by straight, brown hair, mine long, his short. Will was ten months younger than me. Right now we were the same height although Mom said that would change any day soon. Unlike me, Will had huge feet and was destined to grow as tall as Dad. I looked at Will and knew I saw my own expression. His face was pale and unhappy, tight with the effort of not showing tears. No way we'd go soft in front of the whole town.

We heard the rumble of the cars before we saw them. They were meant to transport coal to the surface, but in an emergency, an empty one might carry accident victims and rescuers.

The first car emerged from the shaft into daylight. Inside was the rescue team. I scanned the men carefully. Dad wasn't among them. The pleading got faster in my head. *Please let Dad be okay. Please. Please.* I stood up to get a better look at the next car, just coming into sunlight.

There was something in the second car. Something not moving. My stomach twisted. I thought I was going to throw up. The something was covered by blankets, so we couldn't see a face or limbs, just lumps. It could mean only one thing: a dead body. Hot tears blinded my eyes.

The third car came into view. I wiped my tears on my sleeve so I could trust my eyes. There was Dad, sitting plain as day between two miners, taller than either of them. The cars jerked to a halt and the two rescuers wrapped their arms around Dad to help him out. He was covered in black dust, but it was Dad. His eyes sought us out in the crowd, and he grinned and waved when he found us.

Will and I ran under the blockade, past the company officials, and right into his arms, Mom a step behind.

We kissed and laughed and hugged each other. We even hugged the miners behind Dad. I'd never felt such a mixture of happiness and relief all at the same time. It made me want to be a church bell, ringing out good news.

"You're alive." I must have rung it out twenty times, touching him to make sure.

"I won't be if you don't stop that poking." He laughed.

Dad. Oh, it was great to have him back. Nothing was sacred to him; everything was grist for the joke mill.

He turned serious only for the telling of the accident. "It's thanks to Nelson I'm alive. Nelson—" We followed his gaze to the motionless lumps in the second car. Dad was a driver and Nelson was his trusted partner, his pit pony. It was Nelson's body they'd brought up, dead under the blankets.

A wave of grief mixed with horror washed over me. Poor Nelson! I'd never had a chance to meet him. I'd only heard years of Dad's stories about him. The pit ponies lived their entire lives below the earth's surface. When Nelson wasn't leading Dad through the deeps or pulling a wagon of coal, he slept underground in a little barn with the other pit ponies. What a cruel twist of fate that he had to be dead to get above ground again.

"Nelson stopped all of a sudden down in the tunnel. I couldn't see, of course, or smell anything out of the ordinary. But Nelson could. I tried to get him to go forward but he wouldn't budge. Next thing I knew the ceiling collapsed in front of him, on top of him. I was trapped, but alive." Dad's voice went quiet. "He took the cave-in on himself."

If a miner came out of the pit alive from an accident, there was usually a pit pony to thank for it. If there were an after-world for animals, I knew Nelson had gone there. *Thank you, Nelson,* I called silently. *Thank you for saving my dad.*

Supper that night was a celebration. Mom decided to make lemon pudding, Dad's favourite dessert. Lemons and butter and sugar cost almost as much as a new pair of shoes, but who could put a price on Dad's life? I separated the yolks and beat the egg whites stiff and high with air.

The smell of a sweet lemony heaven began to fill our kitchen, and we were shooed away so Dad could take a quick bath before dinner. For once, Will and I didn't argue. We waited outside for a few minutes, then stole back on tiptoe to peek from behind a curtain at our father, miraculously alive. To our amazement we saw our parents playing like kids. Dad sat in the big tin tub, and Mom tickled and scrubbed his back. Dad splashed her. She poured cold water over his head. He roared, laughing, as he grabbed her, trying to pull her into the tub with him.

I was glad to see my parents happy, but I couldn't get the sight of Nelson's lumpy body lying under blankets out of my head. There'd been that one second I'd convinced myself it was Dad's body, curled up and still.

My dream of flying and leaving the Island grew a little bigger that night in our kitchen. No way was I going to end up like my mom, running at the sound of that siren, scrubbing the coal dust and the fear of an accident off the backside of a miner.

No siree, Bob. They were crazy to live like this. I'd take my adventures a thousand feet above the ground any day.

CHAPTER 3

My mother would call my dream an obsession if she knew how often I thought about it—all the time.

I know exactly when my dream was born. It came to life seven years ago, on the first Saturday in September 1936. I had just turned six. With my big cousin Caleb, I had gone to play on the cliff overlooking the Atlantic. We were acting out the latest mining accident, the one in which Savino's dad, Vince Calabrese, got his hand mangled. I was lying on the ground, pretending to be badly injured under a runaway coal car.

"It looks bad," Caleb said. "We're going to have to amputate."

Suddenly, from the ocean we heard the buzz of a motor coming closer and closer. Caleb scanned the waves for a boat, but I was looking up. Something strange was coming toward us out of the sky.

"A plane!" I screamed, jumping to my feet.

We watched it zoom overhead, nose down, engine sputtering.

"It's going to land. Look, it's going down!"

After a long minute, we heard a loud crack. The small airplane had ploughed through forty feet of muck until it stuck, throwing the nose forward and the back up. The plane had jolted to a stop hundreds of yards away from us on the far side of a bog. We ran to help, watching in astonishment as the pilot climbed out of the cockpit and fell dizzily to the ground.

Two fishermen must have been watching too. They ran up the path from the beach below, reaching the pilot before we did. They pulled him to his feet, holding onto his arms to steady him.

"You're one lucky devil!" they said.

The pilot took off his goggles and helmet. Long, curly hair cascaded down. It wasn't a he. It was a she—a woman! A small trickle of blood began to ooze down the side of her face, but even so, she was amazingly beautiful. I must have cried out in astonishment for she turned from the men at her sides and stared at me.

"I'm Mrs. Markham," she said with a slight accent. "I've just flown from England."

She spoke directly to me. I felt as if she'd flown across the Atlantic expressly to meet me. By calling herself a "Mrs." she could have been one of my mother's friends, but she was like none of the women I knew in Last Chance Bay. I was tongue-tied.

"From England?" one of the men sputtered. "Alone?" He looked up at the plane as if expecting a man to appear. "That's impossible."

She bristled. "You're wrong. It *is* possible to fly west to east across the Atlantic. I've just proved it."

And she had. She made it by five hundred yards, landed in a bog, and walked out with a gash on her forehead. We later learned she'd set a new world record.

My dream was born right then and there. I turned to Caleb and said, "I'm going to do that one day. If she can do it, so can I. I'm going to fly a plane."

"Right." Even then Caleb took me seriously. He didn't laugh but answered with a determination equal to my own, "And I'm going to discover dinosaur bones just like Joseph Tyrrell did in Alberta. There's more than coal under us."

The miners had a heyday with Beryl "Bog" Markham. They joked about her for months and years after. "That's a woman driver for you," they said. But I paid no mind. I knew better.

Beryl Markham didn't spend five minutes in Last Chance Bay. She took the first plane out, heading for the glamour and adoring crowds of New York. I didn't mind that either. Her visit had changed me forever.

Of course, Will, my little brother, tried to snap the wings off my fledgling dream. He spoke with the voice of everybody we knew in Last Chance Bay. "Who do you think you are? You're a girl. You're poor. Beryl Markham was a rich lady. A miner's daughter can't afford to fly."

Most days I hated Will. He suffered from headaches. The doctor called them migraines. Most days I thought of Will and Jason MacDonald, the school bully, as Last Chance Bay migraines. If you asked me, those boys had imaginations as rat infested as the coal mines they couldn't wait to work in.

"I will too learn to fly. Just you watch me. Amelia Earhart wasn't rich. She did it and so can I."

If Beryl Markham was the spark for my dream, Amelia Earhart was the fuel. Over the next months, I began to hear Amelia's name and see her picture everywhere. Amelia Earhart, America's sweetheart aviatrix, was planning to set a new world flying record. It was the most dangerous flight anyone, man or woman, had ever attempted.

I tucked Amelia's picture into my mirror's wooden frame. She wasn't beautiful like Beryl, but nice looking in a boyish way, more like me. And she wasn't rich. She'd worked as a secretary to pay for flying lessons, and if she could find a way, there was hope for me.

For months we followed Amelia Earhart's preparations for her long flight east around the world. She'd have to stop frequently to refuel and sleep. We listened on the radio the day she took off from California with her navigator, Fred Noonan. Their plan was to be back home in two months. We cheered for them and marked the day on our calendar: May 21, 1937. For six weeks I was glued to our radio with a map Dad made for me. Like the rest of the world, I was eager for the latest news of her odyssey. I marked every leg of her journey with a red pencil line. After she had flown twenty-two thousand miles, I had over two dozen dots on my map to mark her stops across South America, Africa, India, then Australia. On July 1, 1937, they left New Guinea for the last leg over the Pacific Ocean.

On July 2, Amelia and Fred radioed their last transmission saying, "… gas is running low," then they disappeared. My red pencil line stopped with them, somewhere over the Pacific. I didn't put an X or a question mark or a circle to mark the spot. I wanted that line to continue home again to California.

Everyone believed Amelia crashed and died seven years ago. A great hero wouldn't disappear like that, now would she? I knew she'd found her way to an island and survived. Even after she disappeared, whenever I looked at her picture on my mirror, she still whispered to me saying, "Never give up, Meg. You'll do it."

So my obsession thrived, even in Last Chance Bay. Not a day went by that I didn't dream of flying, and I thanked Amelia not for her recipes of tragedy showed in her eyes. How did she do it? Where would I hide my tragedy if Dad had died in the accident instead of Nelson? Every week we heard more and more bad news about the war on the radio. The war was fought in Europe but Canadians and Americans were fighting in it too. Some days it seemed to me as if the whole world were living beside a mine, waiting for the company siren to go off.

Whenever Miss MacKinnon interrupted my daydreaming, she tipped her head forward as if she were trying to catch my thoughts.

"Meg, could you please check the little ones' printing for me?" Gentle, even as she pointed the sword of her pencil.

I nodded, and moved to the front. My littlest cousin, Charlie Wishart, sat on the left.

Charlie was Caleb's youngest brother, almost six. His eyes blinked crazily as he squeezed out a capital R that looked more like a Q. His page was a mess. Sticks and circles smudged under his dirty hand. His tongue worked at the corner of his mouth. His mother, my aunt Beth, had tuberculosis and was always sick. My little cousins enjoyed the results of a hot bath only on Sundays when they visited our house, and poor Charlie got the last of the bath water. Six years of Last Chance Bay coal dust lay crusted in Charlie's skin and not even my mother's vigorous scrubbing could get it out.

For a second, I felt a hot flash of frustration. How could I help Charlie? Our former teacher, Mr. Panzorire, used to pick up sloppy work by his fingertips and burn it in the cast-iron stove. Mr. Worth, before him, would have strapped Charlie's dirty little hand. My hands automatically hid in the pleats of my skirt, remembering my own lessons in survival.

Miss MacKinnon smiled at me confidently. The day she'd set foot in this classroom she'd told us, "From what I gather, I'm sure I'm nothing like your other teachers. If you learn one thing from me, it will be the spelling of *encouragement.* Buried within that word is the key to life."

So I knelt beside Charlie. Without stopping his work, he peeked at me. "How'm I doing, Meg?" he said. Blink, blink.

"Oh … wondrous fine, Charlie."

Even with my lie, his tongue returned to worry his lips. There was a stain of red jam at the corner of his mouth, and my hands itched to wipe it clean.

I couldn't stand it. "Come with me, Charlie. I'll tell you a story while we get you washed up."

At the back, by the stove, I poured a basin of warm water. Charlie soaked his hands obediently, then splashed water around his mouth.

"When I was wee like you, I made up stories for every letter. Here's the one I had for R." I fixed my index finger on a page of air. "One day after it *rrrr*ained, a hungry robin found a worm, but the worm dove down, into the ground—"

Charlie giggled.

"Back here, above the ground," I returned my finger to where I'd started, "the robin wasn't fooled. He gave a little hop," I drew a half circle, "and poked his beak into the ground." I drew a sharp little line to the right.

"Did he get the worm?" Charlie chirped, drying his hands on my skirt.

He placed a clean trusting hand in mine, and I led him back to his desk.

"Yes siree, Bob. He did."

"I'm Charlie. Not Bob."

"It's just a silly thing I say. Like rightie-o. Shall we start on a fresh page?"

His eyes went round. "But we mustn't waste paper, Meg."

"Every new story deserves a fresh page."

Charlie nodded. His lips worked silently as he

repeated the story. "Clever robin." He laughed, finishing a wobbly but unmistakable R.

Beside Charlie, Sally MacEachern sat waiting to hug Miss MacKinnon. Sally was left-handed, and she angled her book on her small wooden desk in the most fantastic way. Miss MacKinnon was the only teacher, the only person in all Last Chance Bay, who didn't worry about left-handedness.

Jason MacDonald's father, the school trustee, had come in to visit one day last September. He wasn't the inspector, but he acted like one, strutting stern-faced up and down the narrow aisles. The wooden floor creaked under his feet. He stopped beside Sally MacEachern. He pulled the pencil from her startled hand and angled her book the proper way.

"What are you doing, girl?" he thundered. "Writing with your left hand will take you straight to the gates of hell."

Miss MacKinnon walked quickly between the rows and wedged herself between them. "It's not the devil's work nor will it stunt her growth," she said firmly.

The room grew quiet. We stopped working and watched with great interest as the most opinionated man in town and the new teacher stared one another down.

"She will write with the hand that wants to do the writing," Miss MacKinnon insisted. There was only a slight quiver in her voice.

"Harrumph." It was the first and only time anyone, especially a woman, had contradicted him. Mr. MacDonald shoved the pencil into Sally's right hand and forced her fingers to close around it.

Sally whimpered.

"She'll write with the God-given hand I tell her," he shouted at Miss MacKinnon.

Two bright pink spots appeared in Miss MacKinnon's cheeks. I was afraid for her. But I was more afraid for Sally.

Maybe Miss MacKinnon felt the same way. After a little silence she nodded curtly at him. "Good day to you then, and thank you for your visit," she said.

I wondered if she had a problem with her hearing. She sounded as if she thought he'd said he was about to leave.

"We all have a great deal of work to do, I'm sure," she said, pointedly. Then, completely ignoring him, she walked away to examine Anna Calabrese's work in the next row.

Mr. MacDonald straightened his tie and glared at all of us. We immediately lowered our heads, pretending to work. Mr. MacDonald marched around the room one last time, his footsteps beating on the floor like a drum, and left.

Without a word Miss MacKinnon returned to Sally's desk and whispered something in her ear. None of us could hear what she said, but it made Sally stop crying, and the next time I looked, Sally had the pencil back in her left hand.

Since that confrontation, Sally had hugged Miss MacKinnon six times a day for letting her write with her left hand.

"Shall we stop lessons for the day?" Miss MacKinnon's heels tapped lightly on the wooden floor. She took her place at the front of the small wood-framed room. I returned to mine. "I read an interesting article in the Boston *Herald* that I want to tell you about."

She was smiling. She had our complete attention even though I had to work extra hard to ignore Jason. He was chewing his nails off and spitting the ends on the floor between us.

I wished Caleb were beside me to clout Jason over the head. Jason respected Caleb. Everybody did. Thinking about Caleb made me mad and sad.

Caleb said he'd gone to work in the mine "temporarily" to help his family in February. Here it was May. Caleb's dad was back at work, but Caleb wasn't back at school. Meanwhile, Miss MacKinnon had taught us all about Odysseus, the greatest hero of the ancient world, and Caleb had missed out. Odysseus had survived ten years at sea determined to make his way home. That's what convinced me that Amelia Earhart could do it too. That's the stuff heroes were made of. Caleb was never going to meet Odysseus down in the pit.

Miss MacKinnon's voice broke through the dreams in my head. "… so scientists think there might have been just one land mass millions of years ago, a super continent they call Pangaea."

Pangaea. It sounded ancient and full of mystery. Very Greek or Roman.

"Were there dinosaurs, Miss?"

"I imagine that was the time of the dinosaurs. Maybe before the dinosaurs. It's a theory. A smart guess."

"I don't believe it," scoffed Jason. Some of the girls in Last Chance Bay had set their marriage hopes on him. What was the matter with everybody? Sure he was well built. If you thought like a cow and wanted a bull.

"Why's that, Jason?"

"It's not in the Bible. Nothing about Panga-banga."

Just once, I wished Miss MacKinnon would swing a real sword and Panga-banga *him*.

"You're remembering Genesis. The theory of Pangaea doesn't contradict the Bible. God separated the earth from the sky and the land from the sea. Sounds remarkably like the land was one big continent, doesn't it?"

Small, handsome Savino was usually quiet and easy-going but the idea of Pangaea provoked him. "But how'd the continents get separated and with such different shapes?"

Miss MacKinnon moved beside the large world map, the first thing she'd hung on our school wall last September. "Fault lines tore apart Pangaea. Millions of years passed. All those jungles decayed into layers of peat. Pressure transformed the peat into coal. The oceans moved between the land. If you look at the coastlines—look at the west coast of Africa and the east of the Americas—they look like puzzle pieces that might fit back to form …"

She looked at us expectantly, waiting.

It was a whisper down the rows. "Pangaea."

"And now before I dismiss you, I want to remind you of the public-speaking contest in another month. It will be held on our last day of school, June 23. Will anyone be seeing Caleb Wishart tonight?"

All the boys nodded. Jane Watson blushed a hopeful red. She'd had a crush on Caleb since his voice turned deep and husky a couple of years ago. She sat directly in front of Jason. Unseen by Miss MacKinnon, Jason reached forward and pulled Jane's bra strap, twisting it in his fingers while Miss MacKinnon spoke.

"Tell Caleb he's welcome to speak in the contest even though he's missed the last months of school. Tell him to come in and see me."

Caleb in the mine. Such a huge mistake. Both Uncle Art and my dad had come close to death in the last four months. Weren't things getting a little too close to home? Caleb was being a beam head. There were more than a few things I wanted to tell him if he ever saw the light of day.

CHAPTER 5

Waves. Hundreds, thousands of them. Wave after relentless wave. The Atlantic battered our coast day and night. Seams of coal below us fueled our lives, but Miss MacKinnon insisted that by understanding the motion of waves we would find freedom. Lordy, adults spoke in a mystery. What did she mean? Did she mean that if I couldn't fly away, those waves would take me? Much as I loved Miss MacKinnon, I knew better. An undertow would drag a girl out, give her a hard time, and then those waves would spit her right back into Last Chance Bay.

I'd brought my four younger cousins and Will to the cliff. It was my favourite spot in Last Chance Bay—a cliff of granite overlooking the Atlantic. The flat top covered in green moss and bushes made a natural stage. Sometimes we were even graced with a curtain of grey mist. With or without a curtain, I directed the world's greatest stories on our stage. The gulls clapped their wings and screamed for encores.

"Please, Meg. Why can't we play Amelia Earhart?"

"Because you always kill her."

It was Sunday afternoon after church. My father and Caleb were digging a vegetable garden. They hoped to start some tomatoes now that the frost was gone.

My mother was taking care of Aunt Beth. "She's poorly today," Mom had said. "I'll do her cleaning and you take the little ones out for some fresh air."

My mother had a habit of dressing up a situation to make it look better than it really was. I wouldn't call Aunt Beth's situation poorly. I'd call it a disaster. At the mine when there was a disaster, the siren wailed and the whole town went running. Aunt Beth had her own kind of siren, and it sure kept my mother and me running. Every Sunday we hotfooted it over to Aunt Beth's to do piles of laundry, clean the house, and prevent Aunt Beth and Uncle Art from killing each other. Almost as deadly as the tuberculosis that consumed her, Aunt Beth also suffered from a sharp tongue.

Most of the men in Last Chance Bay worked six days a week in the mine. Rich or poor, they saved the seventh day for church and family. Most of us had a garden on the protected side of the house since not much grew on the side where the wind arrived first. Uncle Art should have been tending his own garden, but he was sleeping off Saturday night.

Every night was Saturday night to Uncle Art, if you asked me. I never saw him without a drink in his hand "to relax." Dad said the mine had got to Uncle Art. Dad said it was hard to raise five children in a tiny company house on a tiny miner's wage. Mom said it was harder to watch your husband drink it away. I said nothing. It was obvious Last Chance Bay had got to both of them. Aunt Beth was like the flour-bag curtains on a south-facing parlour window. Even the words *Robin Hood* had faded away. She sat in her rocker by the kitchen stove coughing up blood and instructions to my cousins, while Uncle Art snored upstairs in bed.

Sunday morning I prayed for Aunt Beth and Uncle Art, and then for me. I reminded God and the saints in heaven that since I already had two big problems in my life—being a girl and living in Last Chance Bay—I didn't want "poorly" as a third. Save me, Saint Amelia, from tuberculosis. It was more contagious than working in the mine.

"We won't kill your Dear Heart this time, we promise."

"It's Earhart." I corrected wee Charlie for the hundredth time. I looked into his blinking eyes. All my cousins had Uncle Art's fair, freckled skin, but only Charlie had his red curls. I loved him, but he was the spitting image of his father. I felt he needed me to be hopeful for him.

"No. Let's continue Odysseus from last week. Where'd we end up?"

Sandra, who was eleven and the eldest of the four, said, "We jumped out of the horse and killed all the Trojans. We're supposed to set sail for Greece, but Dad hasn't repaired the hole in our skiff."

"We need a storm so we can play a boat sinking," Stuart argued. He was ten months younger than Sandra and hated being in the middle of the family.

"It's blue skies today. I say we do Amelia." He looked at Will for agreement.

Will nodded.

"Charlie and I can be stowaways," piped up Nancy. She was nine, closer in age to Stuart, but he was too argumentative so she always paired off with her youngest brother, Charlie.

"I'll be the radio announcer," Will offered, "and Sandra can be Amelia."

I stared at my brother, trying to read his motives. Will was bolder than the Greeks. He kept his face as impassive as a horse. Against my better judgment, I agreed.

"All right, Will. If you're the radio announcer, they'll take their cue from you. You can land Amelia's plane on an island, on a reef, on a whale if you want, but there is to be no crashing, no blowing up, no sinking. Got it?"

Will nodded again, the ghost of a smile around his mouth. Sandra went to the prop pile and donned an old miner's helmet, now an aviator's cap. I picked up a long plank and balanced it across her shoulders for wings.

"Stuart," I ordered, "you be Fred Noonan, the navigator."

Stuart guided them onto the runway, then

hopped in beside Sandra. Charlie and Nancy crouched behind them, hiding. The sky waited overhead, a deep, beckoning blue.

Will, the announcer, sat on a rock and held his hands over his ears like earphones. "Hello, America. This is Will Christie, live from Oakland, California, where we're keeping you posted to Amelia Earhart's unbelievable trip around the world. We are hours away from another world-record-breaking trip. We've just contacted the U.S. Coast Guard cutter *Itasca*. Come in, *Itasca*."

I positioned myself at the edge of the cliff.

"Where are you, *Itasca*? Come in."

I shouted back, "We're off Howland Island."

"How are the plans for takeoff? Have you heard?"

Sandra and Stuart gave a thumbs-up from their plane on the runway.

"Oh, yes. Amelia just radioed us. They're fueled up and on the runway, ready to leave New Guinea at precisely midnight."

Will shouted with excitement. "Did you hear that, America? In exactly two minutes Amelia Earhart will fly the last seven thousand miles of the first-ever flight round the world piloted by a woman. That's right, a woman. The incredible, the invincible Amelia Earhart."

Why did Will always manage to make Amelia into a circus act?

"Where does this woman find her courage? Just imagine, America, flying through the worst storm of the year. All you can see is rain beating down on your cockpit window and whitecaps of the Pacific Ocean ready to drown you below. And imagine a few sharks' fins—"

I slashed a big "cut" signal through the air with my hand. *No sharks*, I mouthed.

Will grinned. "Thirty seconds left, America. Get ready for the countdown. They've flown twenty-two thousand miles already, from Florida to Africa and India, and there's only one more bit, to California. The President of the United States himself intends to meet them. And here's the countdown: ten, nine, eight …"

Sandra, Stuart, Charlie, and Nancy made engine noises and stamped their feet wildly on the rocks. It made me nervous.

"Stay away from the edge!"

"… three, two, one. Take off, America! It's 00:00 hours, Sunday, May 28, 1944—"

"Not today's date you idiot! Why'd I ever let

you be the announcer? It's July 2, 1937." Was I the only one who remembered?

"Geesh," he grumbled. "Amelia Earhart is on her way back to California!"

Sandra, Stuart, Charlie, and Nancy ran back and forth across the rock. The wind off the Atlantic was strong and their wooden wings dipped dangerously from side to side.

I had a terrible thought. What if the wind gusted under the board and they held onto it and flew for a second out over the rocks and waves fifty feet below—

"Sit down," I hollered. "You can look down on the waves and pretend you're flying over the Pacific. Let's cut to the last transmission. Remember? Amelia calls in as KHAQQ."

Will gave me a dark look. I'm sure he was wishing disaster on my Amelia, strong winds, hungry sharks, and hundred-foot rogue waves. Boys!

Sandra followed my suggestion and called on her radio. "KHAQQ calling *Itasca*. We must be on you but cannot see you … gas is running low …"

The Coast Guard didn't get a chance to respond. Will jumped up, waving his arms for everyone in the plane to move.

"Mayday. Mayday," he screamed.

Sandra, Stuart, Charlie, and Nancy obeyed his signals and stood up in the plane.

"They're out of fuel and falling. They can't get the raft out. There are stowaways blocking the exit."

Sandra, Stuart, Charlie, and Nancy started pushing each other around the plane.

"Be careful," I yelled at them.

"They're running out of time. They're going to crash into the Pacific Ocean if they don't get that raft—"

"Cut!" A scream rose from the pit of my stomach—when a boy's laugh stopped me.

I knew that laugh. I turned around.

It was Caleb.

He was leaning against his bike, just where the path from the road ended at the grassy stage. His straight dark hair needed a trim and flapped in the wind. He had a scar over one eyebrow that went red when he was angry. It rarely turned red. Something was different about him today. The mine had been changing him, and I hadn't noticed until now. He was still skinny, but his chest looked broader. He looked older, almost a man. He stood there against his bike, squinting at the sun, laughing at us.

"Cut" turned to "Caleb." I wanted to talk to him, but I also wanted to turn back and rip Will's earphones off.

Will wailed his last line.

"She's crashed. She's down, folks. In the Pacific. All hope is gone—"

I looked back at the edge of the cliff where my cousins had been. There were only tufts of tall green grass bowing in the wind. My heart sank. Darn that Will. Amelia's last flight had gone over the edge.

CHAPTER 6

Caleb was a step ahead of me, running to look over the edge of the cliff.

The plane—Sandra, Stuart, Charlie, and Nancy—had crash-landed on a wide rocky ledge that protruded five feet below us. With an old tube of bright red lipstick that he'd scoffed from Mom's bag, Will was applying blood to Sandra's forehead with a generous hand.

"Amelia's hurt bad. Get a doctor."

Out of character, Sandra opened her eyes. "How are you going to get a doctor when we're stranded in the Pacific Ocean?"

I longed to be close enough to smack them both. "I've told all of you a million times not to go on that ledge. It's not safe."

Fearless Caleb jumped down beside them. "I'm a doctor. Just here in the Pacific to do a little ocean fishing."

It had been too long since Caleb had played with us. I nearly burst out laughing.

"They weren't supposed to crash," I cried. "Please, Caleb. They shouldn't be on that ledge in this wind."

No one was paying attention to me. For a few seconds I entered a strange time warp. I became six again, listening to the radio, and the announcer was saying, "Amelia Earhart's gone!" I'd pounded the wooden radio cabinet trying to stop those words.

Bending down, Caleb gathered a giggling Sandra in his arms. Back in character, she closed her eyes and flung out a pale limb.

Caleb picked her up, saying, "Amelia first. Up we go. The rest of you follow me."

Caleb carried Sandra up a narrow path to the top and laid her gently at my feet. What was she, a peace offering?

No way. They had no brains and no feelings,

killing off Amelia like that. They knew I revered her. Was it so hard to respect?

"Here she is, Meg. Amelia Earhart."

Something exploded in me. I clapped my hands. "Playtime's over. Everybody to the swimming hole to get cleaned up."

"But it's freezing!" Stuart complained.

"You'll have to make do with cold water. I'm not drawing baths for you lot. Sandra, scrub that lipstick off your face. And then it's my house for supper."

Charlie groaned.

"All right. Stay filthy for another week. Why should I care? You can explain yourselves to your poor mother."

Sandra put her cap away but stared at me with sorry eyes. Stuart started to move in the direction of the swimming hole, glaring.

"Aw crap. What's the big deal?" he muttered. "Amelia Earhart *did* crash."

Will exploded at me. "What are you so mad about? It could've been worse. We could've killed her."

"I told you no crashing."

"You're too bossy to have any fun with."

He took one look at my face and started running. The others chased after him.

I picked up a rock, aiming to throw it. "Boys! Murderers! You're all the same!"

Caleb reached out and put his hand on my wrist. His palm was hard and scratchy.

"Don't." I yanked my wrist away and hurled the rock out over the ocean.

"You can't kill your own brother," Caleb said, laughing.

"Give me one good reason why not."

"He's my cousin."

Caleb knew I worshipped the *terra firma* he walked on, but I was mad. "Will's got no feelings. He knows what Amelia Earhart means to me. He's going to grow up like the rest of the boys in Last Chance Bay. He'll get some poor girl pregnant and make her a miner's wife. Or he'll take off on some glorious adventure and leave her stuck here. Why don't I do us all a favour and knock him off right now."

Caleb leaned over, his expression quizzical. "What's wrong, Meg? Jason giving you trouble? Just tell me and I'll set it straight with him."

My heart flip-flopped. Why did Caleb have to be my cousin? It was incense—or some word like that—to like a boy in your own family. I'd overheard something about that in a sermon and looked it up in the dictionary. I'd found the word *incense*, something you burned to smell sweet, from the Latin *incendere*, to set fire. There was a fire in my heart for Caleb, but I was praying no one had noticed the smoke.

"Aw, Caleb." Against my will, tears leaked into my eyes. I blinked ten times to stop them. I didn't want Caleb thinking I was a baby. It was bad enough being more than three years younger. And related.

I swiped the back of my hand across my face.

"Dirt road." Caleb reached out and traced a finger down my dirty, wet cheekbone. "You should have played Amelia, you know. You were always a great Amelia."

A million questions burst out all at once.

"Did you talk to Miss MacKinnon? Don't you miss school? How is it? Down in the mine, is it—"

"Whoa, Meggy-bells. What do you want to know first?"

"The mine. Do you like it?" How many times had I waited for my dad at the gates, watching the men leave their shift, and wondered about the mine? What was it like down there? It was a place of mystery, a place I'd only heard stories about.

"Like it?" He laughed but looked away. "It's not a place you like. I like the men. And I don't mind hard work. But the mine? It's not what I'd thought. Imagine the darkest night when there're no stars or moon. And there's a smell …" He paused again, searching for words.

I knew the smell he was talking about. I smelled it in my father's lunch pail and on his mining clothes when he brought them home once a week for my mother or me to scrub to a dull grey. I hated that smell. It was the smell of the underworld, of closed-up rocky spaces that have been exploded apart against their nature.

"Imagine you wake up from a dream and it's totally dark around you. Ever had that happen?"

I hugged myself. Waking up like that terrified me. "You don't know if you're awake or in a nightmare."

"You have to control the panic that starts. Maybe it's like being blind. No. I think it's worse. Down there it's not only dark, it's under the earth and sky. It's not our world. It's suffocating … a suffocating dark."

He shook his head slightly and his brown bangs flipped back. "But the miners are great. It helps knowing they're down there with you. They sing and … Hey, let me give you a ride to the swimming hole. We'll take the road."

Just like that he stopped talking. He walked to the road and straddled his bike, waiting for me. I climbed side-saddle on the crossbar in front of him. I'd sat there other times, other years, but this time, something was wrong. I was uncomfortable. His arms on either side of me were covered with brown hair and freckles, and the muscles under his skin pulled tight as he steered us, bumping, down the rough road. My head bounced slightly, hitting his chest, and I could smell the soap they used in the showers at the mine. He smelled like my dad. Green trees and bushes flew past.

Usually I held onto Caleb's arms, but I knew I'd die if I did that today. I grasped the metal handlebars, inches from the skin of his hands.

"If Jane Watson sees us, she won't speak to me for a week. Or you."

Caleb's face came in close beside mine. His voice was soft in my ear. "Who cares about Jane Watson."

My body started doing something very strange. Humming. My skin was singing. I was in a new world, there inside the small orbit of Caleb's arms. If he took his hand off the handlebar and put it around my waist … I was in agony … hoping … dreading. I wanted it to last forever. I wanted it to stop. It was scary. Thank God the path to the swimming hole was only a few hundred feet ahead. We stopped and I leapt off the bike, wrenching myself away from Caleb. The humming was less insistent but still there. I wrapped my arms over my chest to hold myself together.

"You and Jane Watson might as well be engaged. She's moony over you, Caleb. Especially since you started working. It's Caleb this and Caleb that. You're a hero, better than Miss MacKinnon's Odysseus."

"Jane'll get over me. Soon as one of the other boys, like Jason MacDonald, goes into the mine, she'll set her cap on a new peg." Caleb's voice had turned harsh. His face was a closed book.

The humming in my skin stopped. The world came into focus. Brown dirt of the road. Green bushes beside us. What had I said wrong?

"I didn't mean anything," I apologized. "I just think you should know that Jason seems interested in her."

Caleb's face relaxed. "As you always said, if you've got no imagination, you deserve what you get."

I laughed. We were back on normal ground. I unwrapped my arms from my chest. "Come for a swim?"

"Can't. Garden's dug, but Ma asked if we'd fix the roof. I'm heading over to Savino's to see if his dad has extra shingles."

Vince Calabrese had a shack out back that was crammed full of every building supply imaginable.

"Can't your dad do it?"

"He's still ... you know. He was out last night."

I nodded, knowing exactly what he meant. His family tiptoed around Uncle Art. For good reason. Just before Christmas of 1943, Uncle Art got the news that his brother Stuart had died while fighting the Germans for control of some Italian seaport. Uncle Art had put his fist right through the front door. Left a big hole, a special Last Chance Bay wreath.

"Miss MacKinnon hopes you'll enter the public-speaking contest with the senior students. You haven't quit school forever, have you, Caleb?"

Caleb gave me a strange look. "I don't know, Meg. I'm thinking about it. There're other ways to finish school, you know."

"You mean the correspondence courses?" I was filled with hope that he was considering them. Miss MacKinnon had said they were a good way to work and finish high school at the same time.

Caleb didn't answer. He biked away, and before I joined my cousins to wash up, I turned to watch his checkered shirt grow small and blur into a solid red. It didn't seem so very long ago that he was telling me about dinosaurs and how he was going to make big discoveries when he grew up. I watched him round a bend and then—poof!—the road was empty, just a bit of dust rising from the tracks of his bike.

CHAPTER 7

In the summer of 1939, just before the war started, I was almost nine. For two years since Amelia Earhart's disappearance, I'd carried an inspired but fuzzy image in my head—that's me, Meg Christie, flying a plane! Somehow I'd take up the torch that had fallen with Amelia. How the heck I'd do it, well, I'd figure that out later. But that summer my dream took on a sharper definition, as if I'd focused the lens of a telescope and brought the image a little closer to reality.

It was the third summer that I'd pestered my dad to take me to the Sydney airfield where there were sometimes air shows on Sunday afternoons. That year we were still in what my parents called the Depression. That was one word I didn't have to look up in the dictionary. It meant Dad stayed home without work too many days because the mine was closed. It meant we looked at things in the store windows and the catalogues but didn't ask for them.

When August came, I knew there wouldn't be many air shows left.

"If you won't take me, then I'll go alone," I argued with my dad in the parlour.

"Not in this lifetime, young lady!" my mother called from the kitchen. "You're too young. And a girl can't travel alone to Sydney. It's not safe."

"I wish I were a boy," I muttered, too quietly for my mother to hear. "You'd let Will go if he asked, wouldn't you," I said, glaring at my father.

"We can't afford it right now. I haven't worked for six days straight," Dad said, sounding annoyed. Who was he annoyed at? Me? The company? The world for not buying our coal?

"We went to the circus in July. If we could go to that, why not the air show?"

"We've been through this, Meg. The circus came here. We didn't have to pay for the tramcar."

Sydney was an hour away on a tramcar ride that cost twenty-five cents. Math wasn't my best subject, but I knew how hard it was to earn a quarter. There and back for the four of us would cost eight quarters, a total of two dollars.

"You got any money, Meg?"

I looked in my pocket. It was empty except for a bit of green velvet ribbon I'd found at the dump. Sometimes I had a precious coin or two after blueberry picking. That was long, back-breaking work, all to earn ten cents, my spending money if I wanted to see a Saturday matinee. Shirley Temple had starred in *The Little Princess* at the local movie theatre on the weekend, and my last two nickels had allowed me to cry all afternoon watching it.

It was Caleb who helped me get to Sydney. We were drying ourselves on the rocks after a day of swimming at the beach. The tide was going out and he spied a bunch of crabs caught in a pool below us.

"Whoopee. Those are big ones. I bet Mrs. Harrison will pay twenty-five cents a piece for them." Mrs. Harrison was the manager's wife, and her fine, well-dressed sisters were visiting from Boston. They wouldn't be caught dead catching crabs, but we knew they loved to eat them.

If there was one thing I was lousy at outmanoeuvring it was red, slimy crab claws. Their one mission in life was to snap your finger off. If you were quick and nervy, you could catch them from behind, but I was neither. Their beady little eyes had a hypnotic effect on me. Every time I looked into them, they said slow down … and I obeyed.

"Go find some pails at the dump and I'll catch 'em." Caleb must have read the dazed look on my face.

By the time I got back, he had fourteen big ones dead on the beach. We loaded them in the pails and sold them to Mrs. Harrison and her sisters for a total of $3.50.

"We split it," Caleb offered generously. "Fifty-fifty."

My dream of seeing an airplane was suddenly so close it kept me from doing the right thing. Caleb deserved a bigger share, but I hungered after that pile of quarters in his palm as if it were the sultan's gold.

I thought I caught a flicker of the same look on Dad's face when I spilled seven quarters onto the kitchen table. Dad lit his pipe, drawing on it steadily, chugging out smoke like a human chimney. Slipping his hand in his pocket, he drew out a quarter and held it between us.

"God will have to understand if we're not at church on Sunday and this money doesn't make it to the collection plate." He tossed his quarter on the pile. "What say?"

What say? I was speechless. Day after day, weeks turning into months, then years, we had done without. Mom made our clothes from flour sacks, trying to hide the *Robin Hood* letters in the seam or across the backside of our underwear. None of us ever complained. Now Dad and I looked at that pile of quarters with a pent-up, drooling desire to be carefree. For once, how would it feel to pretend there was an endless source of sultan's gold? To buy new clothes or go to a circus or a movie or the air show in Sydney any time we pleased.

Fact was, I was speechless all the way to Sydney on the electric tram, squished in-between my parents and Will, who grabbed the window seat, and all the way until I stood breathless on the airfield, and a Gypsy Moth biplane came swooping out of the sky, larger and closer, suddenly over us, over the crowd, its bright red wings only a few feet above our heads, the pilot's face close enough that I could see his devilish grin.

Everybody screamed and ran. Not me. I held out my arms hoping to touch the fibre of its wings. Just a little closer, and I could grab on and be carried, finally, up into the sky.

The pilot pulled up and away, dipped his wings, circled, and nosed down to land on the mowed field where we stood. He taxied up close beside us. Motor off, he climbed out and approached to find the one person who'd stood her ground in the field.

"Are you crazy or something, kid?" he yelled. His enormous face and dark, bushy moustache towered over me. "What if I'd crashed on top of you?"

I stared at him, awed. It was God talking to me from a burning bush. I was slightly disappointed that it wasn't a woman, but, holy macaroni, it was a pilot and his plane was thirty feet away and the Sydney airfield was solid under my feet and this was really, actually happening.

My knees wobbled like jelly. I grabbed his leather sleeve.

"A few years ago … I met Beryl Markham," I managed to say. My thoughts were jumbled. "I want to fly …"

He shoved his goggles up on top of his helmet.

Dark blue eyes stared at me with a funny expression. "You got it bad, kid."

I nodded.

"Got three dollars for a ride?" His black moustache wiggled when he talked.

I shook my head.

"What's your name?"

I choked it out.

"Tell you what, Meg Christie. I'm Billy Buzz. You find me ten paying passengers before that storm hits and I owe you a ride. Deal?"

Before my mother could stop us, Billy Buzz hoisted me up on his shoulders. As if my life depended on it, I started imitating the circus barker I'd heard in July.

"Come one, come all. Nothing to be scared of. This is your chance in a lifetime. Take a ride with America's flying ace, the one, the only, Billy Buzz."

My parents and Will watched from the back of the crowd, their mouths hanging open. My mother's lips quickly disappeared into a thin, grim line—a sure sign I was in for trouble.

Billy Buzz had a line-up of eleven paying customers before his shoulders even had time to ache. He returned me, safe and sound, flushed with attention, to my mother's side.

"Meg Christie," she hissed in my ear. "What the devil's got into you?"

"He's going to take me up in his plane," I boasted.

"Over my dead body."

Rigor mortis set into my mother's shoulders. She meant business. But so did I. I was the one who'd die if I didn't go. She'd thank me later. I nodded obediently, trying hard to look sweet and apologetic, like Shirley Temple in the movies.

Thankfully the roar of the plane's engine distracted her. I edged away from her, over beside my father, and lifted my head. The sight of Billy Buzz zipping over our heads chased my mother's threat right out of my head. Red wings were bright against the dark sky. The lucky passenger sitting in front of Billy held onto her hat and waved like a madwoman at us.

What was it like up there? I tried to think how the earth might look. One big stretch of green before the blue of the ocean? It was impossible to imagine. One by one I watched eleven nervous people go up. You never knew what Billy Buzz would do next. Sometimes a loop. Sometimes a nose dive. Once he went right through the open doors of the hangar, in one side and out the other!

Whatever stunt he pulled, eleven smiling people came down. I nearly peed in my pants I wanted to go so badly.

When the first bolt of lightning lit up the sky, the crowd groaned and began to disperse, running in all directions, some to the hangar for shelter, some to their cars parked at the side of the field, hoping to beat the rain that spat on us, ruining our fun.

It was my turn! This was my big moment. After Billy's Moth taxied by the crowd, I broke away from Dad's side and ran as if that lightning were chasing me. I caught up as Billy came to a full stop. Ducking my head under the wings, I popped up beside him and grabbed the plane, ignoring the passenger trying to climb out and past me. For my determination I got a big foot on my elbow and a "Hey, kid, watch out!"

I didn't budge. I *was* watching out. Watching out for my dream.

"It's my turn now, isn't it, Billy?" He hadn't cut the motor so I had to yell over its roar.

Billy grinned and his cheeks puffed under the edges of his helmet and below his goggles, rounder than a baby's bum.

"Bad storm," he yelled, pointing up to the dark

heavens. "This baby's going to the hangar. I'll take you another time, kid. Promise."

Lightning struck my heart. I couldn't breathe for a second. He wasn't going to take me up? Another time? There wouldn't *be* another time. I'd never get back to Sydney. He had no idea how hard this one trip had been.

"Oh, please ..."

There was a real crack of thunder and I jumped, letting go of the plane. Billy waved. With quick reflexes he accelerated the plane away from me.

"Don't worry, kid. A promise is a promise."

Rain started in earnest, filling the little craters in the field with puddles. My parents and Will surrounded me, all talking at the same time. My mother was furious. I was going straight to my room when I got home. I let my parents cover me with a coat. It felt like my funeral.

Will used his favourite line. "Things could be worse."

"Oh yeah. How's that?"

"The plane could get hit by lightning."

I turned and watched the red Gypsy Moth taxi into the hangar, out of my life.

"I wish it would."

It was a cold, soggy journey home on the tramcar. I stared out the window, not knowing if the drops on the thick pane of glass that blurred my vision came from inside or outside. It didn't matter. Life couldn't get any worse. I was as miserable as a body could get.

CHAPTER 8

The beginning of June 1944 and the sun felt like an older cousin you had a big, stupid crush on. It shone warm and close, so close you had to warn yourself it would burn you alive if you dared to touch it.

At home, at least for a few days, we forgot the long winter and the horrible mine. We even forgot about the battles in Europe. The war had been going on so long it reminded me of those years we'd had an awful teacher at school. You got used to it after a while.

Will and I did our chores happily after school until Dad got home from work. With the war, Dad had work at the mine every day except Sunday. A war needed lots of coal.

I couldn't understand the boys in Last Chance Bay who talked about war as if it were a good movie they were saving up to see. One day last December, when my uncle Stuart was fighting in Italy with a lot of other Canadians, Miss MacKinnon read us poems from the Great War. I suddenly had vivid images of soldiers coming back from the trenches—blind or with no legs. Soldiers who had bad dreams and thought war was a pit. Jason must have told his father about those stanzas of soldiers because the next day Mr. MacDonald forbade any more poetry reading at school.

That first warm day of June, I enjoyed the sunshine so much, I even liked taking the wash off the line for my mother. As I folded the clothes I rehearsed the new Latin words Miss MacKinnon had taught us that week. I used *bonus* and *malus* over and over in my head. Today the wind spewed *malus* soot from the big, *malus* smokestack at the mine. All the clothes were dry but a *malus* gray.

You could get fixated on bad things if you weren't careful.

The sun was *bonus*. Dad was alive. I'd see Caleb on the weekend. Very *bonus*.

Mom puttered in the garden beside me, preparing her roses for a glorious summer ahead.

"What do you think, Meg? My roses are every bit as beautiful as those at Buckingham Palace."

"I'd rather be in Buckingham Palace," I said.

Mom's face fell.

"But your roses are … *bonus*." We hadn't learned the word for beautiful yet. She raised her eyebrow. "Latin?"

"It means good. Miss MacKinnon says we need to know the roots of words."

"Leave it all in the basket." Mom sighed. "I'll have to do a wash again tomorrow and hope the wind changes. No sense in doing Beth's wash today."

"We could call it a malicious wind instead of an eastern one. Malicious comes from *malus* too, that's how it got to—"

"That's quite enough. Thank you, Miss MacKinnon."

Mom was proud that I did well at school, but she didn't hold with a girl getting too uppity in her ways. My mother believed a woman's place was in the home. I'd asked a million times if we could invite Miss MacKinnon for dinner, but Mom always found an excuse. She didn't know what Miss MacKinnon liked to eat. Aunt Beth was coming over. The house wasn't clean. I knew without Mom saying it out loud: Miss MacKinnon made her uncomfortable.

Dad got home late for supper that night. He had better than *bonus* news and it anchored us to the table.

"The union's won!" he announced in a booming voice. His grin hung over us like a crescent moon. The union was right up there with God in our lives, fighting the evil working conditions in the mines. We stopped breathing, waiting to learn what we'd won.

Dad kept grinning, enjoying the suspense.

"Won what?" I asked, unable to stand it any more.

"A week's holiday. A paid week's holiday!"

Mom put both hands to her cheeks. She jumped up and rushed to Dad's side, throwing her arms around him. He patted her on the back, raising his eyebrows at us over her shoulder.

"I can't believe the company gave in," Mom said. "A week's paid holiday, after all these years. What made them give in?"

"Hard to say, really. Maybe it's the war. We all need something to look forward to and celebrate."

They kissed. Will kicked me under the table. He hated kissing as much as I hated him.

"Would you rather they fight?" I hissed, kicking him back a good one in the shins that made his eyes tear up. I was just getting him back for crashing Amelia last Sunday.

Will grabbed his fork and catapulted green peas toward me. They bounced off my head onto the floor. I would've clobbered him, but he was annoyingly stronger. Boys! They got all the breaks. We both took after Aunt Beth, with our small faces and sea-green eyes, but there the similarities ended. I was turning into a girl no matter how much I resisted, a girl with long hair and wee breasts not much bigger than those peas.

"So what will we do? Where will we go?" Will asked. I harboured the same question. We'd heard about holidays. I thought they were only for rich people until Miss MacKinnon explained that most working people deserved paid time off in the year to relax and travel and visit family. It was strange to think of the company giving Dad money for a day he didn't go down in the mine.

"Do? Go?" said Dad while my mother carried a fresh pie to the table. "The union's going to organize a community picnic. And one day we could visit your grandmother in Sydney Mines."

Mom thunked the pie on the table. "Visit your mother on our one and only, our very first holiday?" Her hands that had tended a rose garden only an hour ago were now fists on her hips.

Time to put my two cents in. "Why can't we go to Boston or New York?"

"May I remind you that the company is not going to pay for an expensive trip, so you can get that out of your head right now, Meg Christie. We only have a week. It'll be a marvellous week. We'll do something special together. You, Will"—he winked at my brother—"you might be able to look after the pit ponies."

Will's eyes lit up. "How's that?"

"We asked for the pit ponies to get a holiday too. Seems only right, them working so hard and spending their lives in the dark for our sakes."

"Could I come on your last day of work and help bring them out?"

Dad stuck his fork in his piece of pie. "Maybe. Your day will come to work in the mine. No need to rush it, son."

Might as well be yes. What about me? "What will I do for the holiday?"

"As I said, the union is planning a picnic. How about a prize-winning apple pie?"

Dad knew I hated the kitchen. His eyes teased, but I gave him my stoniest look.

"In case anybody cares, I still want to get up in a plane."

Me and my big mouth. I'd said it.

Mom groaned. "Oh, Meg. Leave it be. That was five years ago."

Dad laughed and pushed his chair away from the table. "You haven't outgrown that one? Here's the only way of getting out of Last Chance Bay I can offer you, Meg. Tomorrow after work, I'm going over to McArthur's barn to choose a new pit pony. If you want to come with me, I'll be glad of your company."

Will's mouth opened greedily. The desire to go with Dad glistened on his pink, fat tongue.

"Okay." It wasn't what I really wanted, but the envy on Will's face gave me a keen moment of satisfaction. And who knew? Alone I might wrangle a promise out of Dad.

The next evening Dad and I headed out to choose the new pony. Dad whistled and sang his favourite tunes, some of them in Gaelic. I sang along when I knew the words. We walked past the company houses, way past town, and turned up a path through the woods to McArthur's farm.

Darcy McArthur was in his barn. The smell of animals welcomed us when we entered the shadows inside. It took a few seconds to adjust to the dim light.

"Who's there? Norm Christie and his son?"

This wasn't the first time I'd been mistaken for Will. With my hair tucked in a hat and wearing pants and a loose shirt to hide the peas on my chest, I liked the mistake.

"Hello, Darcy. I've come to pick a new pit pony. This is Meg, not Will, with me. She's got an eye for a good animal."

"Well, why in tarnation don't she wear a skirt if she's a girl?"

Thankfully Dad changed the subject. "Did you hear the latest news? The Allies are almost ready to invade France. Army, Navy, and Air Force. Masses of them are in England waiting for the right time and place to cross the channel. They're keeping the exact time and place a secret."

"Those Krauts got spies in every Commonwealth country and even in the United States. They'll be ready for the Allies. No way they'll give France back without a bloody fight. They built an Atlantic Wall, right? Got bunkers and big guns up on them cliffs overlooking them fancy French beaches. Our boys don't stand a chance."

Dad nodded. "I'd rather go down in the pit than have to land …"

They talked about the war, not noticing me as I moved into the shadowy barn. There were a half-dozen ponies in the stalls. Their dark rumps and tails rippled constantly, disturbing the settlement of flies. I eased myself in and out of the stalls, listening to everything the ponies were saying. Mostly they were nervous. They were small for horses, the same height as me. One raised his back leg, ready to kick if I came too close. All of them swit-swatted their tails as if I were a big fly.

The last pony on the right was different from the others. I knew immediately he was the one. He was grey with a strange marking on his rump: a large black island on a sea of grey hair.

When I patted him, he responded happily to my touch, whinnying with pleasure after I rubbed the spot between his ears. I moved around him, listening. He was patient with me and glad I'd come to visit. When he swished his tail, he seemed to want to disturb the flies for both of us.

Wrapping my arms around his neck I whispered in his ear, "My dad needs a good pony like you to guide him."

I thought about Nelson's dead body under the blanket. I thought of all the mining stories Dad had ever told, the cave-ins, the explosions, the runaway cars. I thought of how Caleb described the suffocating darkness. I had a pang of guilt, asking this poor wee pony to give up the world he knew in order to work with my father. It wasn't really fair. How could he know what the mine was like?

"My dad will show you a little garden down there. It's beautiful. You'll visit it every day."

I was a Judas, betraying him like that. As if those few square feet of garden could be a substitute for meadows and blue sky and a fresh breeze off the Atlantic.

The pony didn't smell my guilt. He seem to consider my request, chewing slowly. The sounds of my father laughing with Mr. McArthur filled the barn. The light filtered around us in shades of brown from the dark ground to the knotted swirls in the wallboards to the golden straw baled beside us.

"The miners will be good to you. My dad's life will depend on you—"

My begging was returned with a nudge of the pony's nose, as if to say, "Enough. I'll do it."

"Dad, over here. I've found him."

Mr. McArthur led the chosen pony outside into the last of the evening's light while he commented, "He's a steady one, that one."

My father examined him carefully. The black island on the pony's rump glistened in the angled rays of the sun.

"I've got a name for him," I said eagerly. "Pangaea."

My father laughed, winking at Mr. McArthur.

But Mr. McArthur choked, "What on God's green earth kind of name is that?"

Bristling, I explained what Miss MacKinnon had taught us about the supercontinent and the origins of coal in Cape Breton.

"Blasphemy!" Mr. McArthur roared. His face turned brighter than the sun setting behind the tall pines. "The world was created in seven days. Just the way it is. What kind of nonsense is that agnostic science-worshipper of a woman feeding you kids? Education from that bit of skirt is going to rot your brains, mark my words. Make you unfit for community and family and church. Might as well send you off to Toronto right now and be done with it." His angry red face glared at me, daring me to defy what he declared was right.

I narrowed my eyes. How dare he criticize Miss MacKinnon! "I'm dying to see Toronto."

Surprisingly, Dad laughed again, easing the tension. "You'll never convince my Meg that Miss MacKinnon is wrong. Mind you, I'm not convinced about using the name Pangaea."

"You asked me to come along and name him. You promised me this instead of—"

I'd gone too far. Mr. McArthur barged in, "See what I mean? Miss MacKinnon's teaching these kids to lose respect."

The pony swatted his tail and looked from me to Dad to Mr. McArthur before moving away in search of fresh grass.

"Now, Meg. We need a name less controversial. Your ma's asked me to stay out of trouble. If I start a fight every time I pick up a load of coal, none of the miners will get a day's work and a day's pay."

Mr. McArthur spat.

Dad's eyes softened. "I need a name to bring us luck down there, Meg. A name to inspire confidence. Something … heroic."

Dad knew my soft spot all right. I loved the name Pangaea, but I'd relent, not for appearance' sake, not for Mr. McArthur, but to bring my dad luck in the pit. A second name came unbidden into my mind.

"Pilot?"

Mr. McArthur nodded approval. Dad cheered. "That's more like it. A pit pony to pilot me out of darkness and trouble."

I was annoyed at Mr. McArthur's pig-headedness and the terrible things he'd said about Miss MacKinnon. Even so, I managed to ignore him and smile back at Dad, then at Dad's new pit pony. Pilot or Pangaea, he was a beautiful pony.

The evening ended with something even better. On the walk home from the barn under the first stars of the evening, Dad took my hand.

"There are lots of pilots and planes at the airport in Sydney. I'll ask around. See if someone knows a way to get you up in a plane. And if there is, I'll take you there myself during the holiday."

CHAPTER 9

Tuesday, June 6, 1944, the most amazing thing happened after school. I was walking home with Bozana and Jane, as I did almost every afternoon, when the siren from the mine went off. Without a word or signal, we turned as if one person and ran down the mining road.

Who would it be this time? I had a superstitious belief about bad things coming in threes. It was unlikely to be Dad or Uncle Art again. That left only one person: Caleb. I didn't want it to be Caleb.

Then my stomach took another plunge. What if it was Pilot? It was my fault he'd gone to work with Dad in the pit. I'd sent him to his doom. Only his second day at work and he was already dead under a blanket. I'd never forgive myself if it were true. I swore to myself I'd never go and pick another pit pony for the mine. Will could do it.

In front of the main gates, I found my mother and Will standing with my father. They were smiling and hugging each other. I felt sick. Pilot had died, and they were rejoicing in my father's deliverance.

"It's happened," my dad said, lifting me off my feet. "We're taking the beaches at Normandy!"

It took a second for the news to make sense. It wasn't Pilot. It wasn't an accident. Normandy was in France. It was the war.

"The Allies, girl. Our forces have landed in France. The invasion's begun."

They'd used the siren for good news! The Allied Forces were trying to free France from German occupation, while on the east side of Europe, the Russian Red Army was beating the heck out of the German Army. A hundred-pound weight—one I'd hardly known I carried—left me and in its place a tingling of hope began at my feet and shimmered right up to my cheeks.

"The tides have turned!" Jason MacDonald's father yelled.

Everybody cheered and talked about the invasion. A hundred and fifty thousand American, Canadian, and British soldiers were trying to liberate France. This morning, as we'd slept in bed on our side of the ocean, soldiers and guns of the Third Reich had fought back wave after wave of Allied soldiers on the beaches of Normandy.

We went home to sit by the radio and wait for more news. We didn't hear how many casualties there were for a few days. Nearly five thousand. The carnage had been the worst on something they code-named Omaha Beach.

For several days at school, Miss MacKinnon had us study the map of Europe. We put little markers on the beaches in Normandy. We measured the miles the Allies faced from those beaches to their next main objective: Paris. Then we measured the miles from Paris to Berlin in order to defeat the Third Reich. It was a long way.

Still, we were full of hope. On Sunday we took a big ham over to Aunt Beth's to celebrate. Uncle Art was halfway through a bottle of moonshine. He poured drinks for the adults, including Caleb.

"A toast to the Allies! May all those Huns goose-step straight to their graves for shooting down Stuart."

All the adults except Aunt Beth took a sip. Aunt Beth jerked back and forth in her chair by the stove. Even in June she was cold. Her eyes had a glassy look and her cheeks were bright red. Her drink sloshed in the glass in her hand, untouched.

"What's the matter? D-Day not good enough for you?"

"It's *you* not good enough for me," Aunt Beth cried. Her voice was all scratchy hoarse as if she'd been screaming before we came. She started coughing. Coughing and hacking into a handkerchief.

"You lousy, good for nothing—" she tried to start again but was stopped by a fit of coughing. Her drink spilled on her skirt.

"Give me that," Uncle Art roared. His hand reached out toward her face, but at the last minute wrenched the drink from her hand. "No sense wasting good drink."

"Stop it, Dad," Caleb said, stepping forward. The scar over his eyebrow was bright red. "You're making things worse."

My dad got to Uncle Art first. "Art. Bring your drink and relax. Let's sit in the parlour and listen to the radio. See if there's any progress."

My dad deftly steered Uncle Art out of the kitchen away from Aunt Beth. I was stiff as a frozen shirt on a winter laundry line. I'd seen Uncle Art hit Aunt Beth before. Why did they have to fight so much?

My mother poured her drink down the drain and filled the glass with water for her sister. She tried to rub her back, but Aunt Beth shrugged her off and turned her face away to cry.

I didn't wait for my mother to shoot me the give-us-some-privacy look. I turned away and walked into the parlour. With nine of us in that small room, it was crowded. No one knew how to liberate the silence that occupied us now. Uncle Art collapsed into a comfortable chair beside the radio, muttering, "Those lousy Huns! Talk about lousy ..."

I glanced at Caleb. He stood at the window with his back to us. His hands were shoved in his pockets; his shoulders were hunched up tight, creating an impenetrable wall between us. He was miles away. I didn't know how to reach him, bring him back.

Will broke the silence. "Who wants to play at the cliff? We'll play the invasion, what do you say?"

"Good idea, son. Get a little fresh air before dinner." My dad's voice sounded tired. Dad put his drink on the mantel and pulled Uncle Art to his feet.

"Come on, Art. What do you say you and I get a little fresh air on the porch? How long before we reach Berlin ...?"

The door slammed shut behind them and their voices faded. I stayed in the parlour, unable to stop staring at Caleb's imposing back. I wanted to pull him by the hand and follow our siblings to the cliff, as we'd always done, but I didn't dare disturb his thoughts.

Slowly I let my back slide down the wall until I sat on the floor next to the radio. I turned it up. General Dwight D. Eisenhower's voice filled the room. They were replaying his D-Day speech to Europe. Eisenhower had a calm voice with a gentle drawl. Miss MacKinnon told us he came from Kansas. It wasn't a passionate speech but I liked it, especially the ending. It gave me a quiet kind of confidence that determination would pay off and the war would end.

"I call upon all who love freedom to stand with us now. Together we shall achieve victory."

Throughout the entire speech Caleb kept his back to me, but I noticed his shoulders gradually relax. He began to sway slightly back and forth on his heels. Outside I could hear Uncle Art and my dad singing Gaelic songs loud enough for all Cape Breton to hear. Dad called it "drowning their sorrows." In the kitchen I could hear my mother and Aunt Beth talking softly, drowning theirs, I suppose. Every now and then I heard the clatter of a pot and the scrape of a knife peeling vegetables. The smell and sizzling sounds of the ham cooking in the oven made my mouth water.

From the radio, a broadcaster's voice explained the week's events with a tally of the casualties. The Allies were facing tough resistance from the Germans. There were battles going on everywhere. It wasn't going to be easy to win France back for the French.

Suddenly Caleb turned around and smiled at me.

"And I call upon all those who love ham to help me round up the hungry hordes."

I pushed myself up, happiness rising out of nowhere. Everything was going to be okay. The

Allies would win the war. Caleb and I would play with our younger siblings for a bit, then bring them home for Sunday dinner.

"Together," I said with a laugh, "we shall achieve victory."

CHAPTER 10

The next day, Monday, Caleb got off work early and joined us at school for the last half hour. Miss MacKinnon was delighted to see him.

"Come in, Caleb. Welcome. I'm just about to explain the rules of this year's public-speaking contest. Perfect timing."

Caleb shuffled his feet uneasily by the door. "I'll stand, Miss."

I guessed what he was thinking. He didn't want to sit in the back row with us because he didn't belong at school any more. He'd enroll in correspondence courses—secretly—that would be Caleb's way. I remembered how he'd cheered up last night. Dinner had turned festive with everyone talking about what they'd like to do for the holiday in August. Dad told everyone he'd promised to take me into Sydney to fly a plane. Everybody laughed and joked, "Is Meg going to be the secret weapon against the Nazis?" But Caleb had whispered to me privately, "It's a deal. This holiday we'll both do something special. Right, Meg?"

I smiled at Caleb as he stood awkwardly at the back of the classroom, remembering our deal, then faced forward to listen to Miss MacKinnon.

"As you know, the school year ends with the public-speaking contest and a community banquet on June 23. I've left the topic of this year's contest a secret until now for a reason. I don't want you to overwork your speeches, because they are to be on the subject of"—she looked at us meaningfully—"passion. Those of you from the senior years who wish to enter must speak about something dear to your heart."

Passion. Didn't Miss MacKinnon use the best words.

"When you choose your subject, remember that our word *passion* comes from the Latin *passus* and in Greek *pathos*. Does anyone know what *pathos* means?"

We all looked at her blankly. I racked my brains thinking of possible synonyms: love, happiness, or maybe excitement?

"It might surprise you to know that *pathos* means suffering. I want you to contemplate that meaning well before you choose your subjects."

She could have told me she was a man in disguise, I was so shocked. How could it not mean happiness? I could follow the roots of *pathos* into the word *pathetic*, but not *passion*. How could the things we were passionate about make us suffer? Something had gone wrong in the English translation.

"Those of you who want to run through your speech with me can arrange to do so before the contest, but otherwise this year's speeches will not be presented to the class in advance. I want you to speak with true emotion and not worry about what anyone else thinks. This is not something that comes easily to most of us."

After school I got my things ready to walk home with Bozana and Jane. Caleb stayed behind to talk with Miss MacKinnon, but he caught my hand at the door before I left.

"I'm taking Saturday off to go into Sydney. Want to work on our speeches in the morning before I go?"

I nodded. My heart leapt to my throat. "Can I come with you to Sydney?"

I immediately regretted asking. Caleb looked uncomfortable. He squeezed my hand, shaking it like a dog's paw.

"It won't work, Meg. Not this time. I've got to … got some, ah, errands to run."

He was still shaking my hand. I could tell he was thinking of a way out. I liked holding his hand but not this way. I felt pathetic, but I'd grovel for my dream if I had to.

"You know I need to find a pilot to take me up in his plane."

He brightened. "I'll ask around when I'm there."

I pulled my hand away. It wasn't as good as going myself. It wasn't as good as spending the day with Caleb. But it would have to do. Caleb would try to help me.

"Meet me on the cliff?"

I nodded.

Outside, Jane gave me a nasty look.

"Kissing cousins?" she teased. "It's called *incest,* Miss Know-It-All, in case you didn't know."

"I do know," I replied, but made a mental note of the word.

"Have you even kissed a boy yet, Meg Christie? Or are you above all that?"

We walked past the big playing field and the community centre. Every Saturday night dances were held here. This was where the school-end festivities would be in less than two weeks.

"I have standards. I'd rather kiss my dad's pit pony than the boys in this town."

I hadn't kissed a boy yet, and I knew darn well she had. Probably Caleb. I hummed "Fascinating Rhythm," a favourite Gershwin tune the band played at every dance.

"It's beyond me why you were born a girl. Which reminds me. I've decided what I'm going to speak about," Jane said, waiting for us to say excitedly *what, what?*

I kept right on humming.

"What? What's your topic?" Bozana asked.

"Women."

Oh, good grief. I stopped humming. What could Jane Watson have to say about women that was the least bit interesting to anyone?

"I'm going to speak about one of my countrymen, a famous Pole," Bozana said.

"Who's that?" I asked.

"You going to teach us how to knit Polack socks?" a boy's voice asked.

It was Jason. Savino was with him. They stepped from behind the community centre, where they'd been smoking out of the wind. Jason's sleeves were rolled up to show off his muscles. He had his eye on Jane. "Or maybe some of those potato pancakes. The Allies could launch them against the Huns." He picked up a rock and hurled it into the woods. "Run for cover!" he screamed. "It's a Polack pancake."

Jane giggled.

As usual, Jason got under my skin worse than Jane did. They were meant for each other.

"And what will you speak about, Jason? Yourself?" I asked.

Jason moved a few steps closer to me, threatening. "I might speak about the union and what happened in 1925 and how my da's getting us our first week's holiday."

"Your dad?" I sputtered. "What's your dad got to do with it? He's the school trustee—and the worst one we've had in years."

"Oh yeah? Says who?"

My dad said, and Caleb said, even my uncle Art said, but I wasn't stupid enough to tell Jason. Jason's dad was a braggart, taking credit for things he didn't do. God help us if he did become the union rep. "All the men say. Why don't you listen? You might learn a thing or two instead of—"

Savino moved between us. "Cut it out. You two might as well be married. You sound just like my parents. Hey! That gives me an idea for what I could talk about: the holy sacrament of marriage. It's where we're all headed. What do you say?"

"As long as you don't make the woman do all the housework," I said quickly.

Jason howled. "And what would you have her do? Become prime minister?" He clapped Savino on the back. Big joke.

"Miss MacKinnon says women should have the same opportunities as men."

He moved the last step closer. He was much bigger than me. It was all I could do to keep my feet firm.

"Miss MacKinnon. We've had enough of Miss MacKinnon. You'll see. Her days are numbered teaching in Last Chance Bay. It's bad enough women got to vote. Next thing you know they'll want to work in the mines. Men's work is men's work. Women!" He sneered. "It's bad luck when women meddle in men's work, didn't you know?"

"That's the oldest, stupidest superstition going. Throw the girl overboard or we'll all drown," I said.

"Maybe you need a lesson in what women are really meant for," he sneered.

Bozana and Jane blushed, staring at me as if I'd crossed some agreed-upon line.

"Looks like we're at the turn-off," Jane said in that singsong, phony voice she put on sometimes. "I'm going to Bozana's. Coming, Meg?"

"No. I've got to get home."

Savino smiled at Bozana. The Polish section of town was right beside the Italian. "Guess I better get home too," he said, grinding his toe over the last of his cigarette. "Come on, Jason."

But Jason shook his head. "Naw. You go ahead without me. I'll just follow Meg here. Make sure she gets home safe."

Savino looked at Jason uncertainly.

"Go on. We need to finish our discussion. See you tomorrow."

Savino hurried to catch up with Jane and Bozana, leaving me alone with Jason.

The tension was thick between us. Now that we were alone, Jason's expression turned hard and nasty. I held Jason's gaze, as bold as I could, but he snickered at me.

I couldn't think of a way out. My tongue felt thick; for once I had no smart remarks. So I turned away, held my head high, and started up the road for home. I heard Jason's steps behind me. I felt his eyes on me. My heart started pounding. Finish our discussion? He meant finish me off.

Why, oh why, did God have to make boys? I reached the shadowy cemetery beside the church and was no longer able to control my feet. I ran between the gravestones straight into the little marsh beyond the church and the next road where I lived. My feet sloshed through wet muck. I lifted my skirt to run as fast as possible, then leapt over the last island at the end of the little marsh. I heard Jason splashing and cursing behind me.

Panting, I crossed the road and reached my doorstep. I turned around to face him, but Jason was nowhere in sight. I slumped against the door with relief.

The smell of roast beef and freshly baked bread reached out to me from inside my house. They were the warm, reassuring smells of dinner, but my stomach was tight with fear. I had no appetite. I hated to involve him, but I had more than the public-speaking contest to discuss with Caleb on Saturday morning. There was no place for a girl to hide from Jason MacDonald in Last Chance Bay.

CHAPTER 11

Saturday morning. I somersaulted out of bed and looked at myself in the mirror. Here's what I saw. Same funny face as always. A pimple on the left side of my nose. Yuck. Today of all days when I was going to meet Caleb. At least there was nothing wrong with my mouth, two ordinary lips. I thought again about Jane's question: have you kissed a boy yet? I kissed the mirror. Misty lips disappeared slowly, the way rain did. My long brown hair was a mess and I shook it into a storm. Wild. Mom said I was the spitting image of her sister, Aunt Beth, before she was married, before Uncle Art and five kids.

I finger-combed my hair into a braid down my back. Now I could see my breasts. To be honest, I hoped I didn't get much bigger, but even prayer couldn't control Nature. Nevertheless, I prayed, *Please God, don't let them pop out too big.* Jane Watson's mother was so big she couldn't see the kitchen floor under her feet.

I remembered what Jane Watson had said on Monday. I looked in my dictionary for the word *incest*. There it was, several words after *incense*. It meant "sexual relations between people closely related, unchaste." Good golly! I slammed the book shut. I wanted nothing to do with that!

Why did Caleb have to be so darn wonderful? I picked out an old shirt of my mother's. It was loose and hid everything. The morning beckoned. I'd work on my speech up on the cliff before Caleb got there. He was a cousin, after all. Nothing to worry about. A distant relation. I intended to impress him. I had it all planned: "Ta-Da! I've decided to talk about Amelia Earhart. Here's my title: How I Survived Seven Years on the Pacific Ocean ... *with passion*."

Caleb would like it. It was the rest of Last Chance Bay I was worried about.

There wasn't a sound in the house; it was the quiet of sleeping. I tiptoed down the edge of the stairs, grabbed some bread out of the breadbox, and was out the front door.

The sky was bright blue. Lots of puffy white clouds. I headed away from the grey houses, up through the woods. How would I persuade the town to my way of thinking? If Odysseus could survive, so could Amelia Earhart. If she were a man, they'd believe in her. What was seven years alone on an island to a hero? The trick would be to take them down through Amelia's last sixty seconds. She'd scan the dark waters below and notice a spot without white waves. It was her only chance. An island ...

I'd reached the shortcut through Mr. McArthur's fields. The strong smell of manure fertilized the air. The fields were strangely empty. Where were the cows? They should have been out, hungry, searching for fresh grass. I tried to concentrate on my speech as I walked carefully up to the back corner, but something nagged at my mind, demanding my attention. I looked around but didn't notice anything unusual until I climbed over the fence. Odd. Someone had lowered the top rail of the gate between the pasture field and Darcy McArthur's woods.

Wouldn't you know it? The cows were there among the dark shadows of the forbidden trees. I watched them for a minute, wondering if I should run over to Mr. McArthur's place to warn him his cows were loose or continue to the cliff to work out the rest of my speech before Caleb came.

A loud bellowing interrupted the peace of the morning. It got louder by the second. Something, someone, was approaching through the woods, down on the right. The cows were every bit as startled as I was and rushed the gate all at once, pushing and bawling to get home as if the devil himself were coming up that hill.

I didn't know what to do. Blood rushed from my heart, trying to revive my brain. I was stuck between escape and wanting to see what was coming. It sounded like a crazed animal. What in tarnation?

It was Gallagher's stud bull. His eyes bulged and his tail stuck straight out. He was heading for us. Right behind him was Jason MacDonald. This was Jason's doing.

Jason saw me. I knew I should run, but still I stood there. Jason's eyes bulged out too, like a crab's, with that hypnotic effect that always immobilized me.

The bull was a huge brute. Slobbery strings of saliva hung from his mouth and he moaned as he charged.

Red-faced, Jason roared, "Yeehaw!" laughing like a lunatic at the sight of the last cows clambering back over the gate.

Except for one small heifer. My heart sank. She couldn't get over the gate rail. She'd managed to clear the lowered rail earlier because it was on the downward slope of the hill, but going uphill was a different story. Twice her size, the bull was closing in on her.

I screamed at Jason, "No. She's too young." The bull would hurt her.

That's when I moved. I pulled the second rail from the top toward me, which released the other end, making it fall to the ground. Scrambling frantically, the heifer cleared the gate.

I ran to the other end of the gate, and with all my strength I lifted and shoved both rails back into place so the bull couldn't follow. On the other side the cows were running safely down their pasture toward home.

The ground shook beneath my feet. Propelled by fear it was my turn to scramble up the gate to get as high as possible. I knew the bull might be scared off by something bigger than him, but the best thing was to get over the fence and keep some distance, at least twenty feet, between us. Bulls had a battle zone and I didn't want to be in it.

I half-turned to see the bull stop and veer away from me and the gate, bellowing his frustration that the cows were gone, but it wasn't the bull I had to worry about.

Jason grabbed my leg before I even knew he'd caught up with me. He yanked and I fell back on top of him.

Yuck. He smelled of booze. Just like my uncle Art.

I rolled and jumped to my feet, disgusted and thankfully more alert than Jason.

He stared at me from the ground. He had a goofy, dazed expression on his face, but I was afraid of him.

There was a short piece of cedar rail on the ground beside the gate, and I grabbed it. It wasn't much of a weapon, but I swung it above my head and stood over him. He pulled his hands over his face protectively and I hollered at him for all I was worth.

"Keep your hands to yourself, Jason MacDonald. What's the matter with you? Haven't you got anything better to do than set McArthur's bull on those poor cows?"

Jason rubbed his head and spoke in a blurred voice, "We been out all night celebrating. My dad and my brothers. I got a job in the pit."

"You call this celebrating?" Jason looked sick to death. For a second I saw the bull's head where Jason's was. Good golly, he smelled awful! My fear exploded up from the pit of my stomach and I threw up all over Jason.

He put his hands up. "Stop … stop." He was covered in the slimy yellow contents of my stomach. It dripped down his hair and over his ears. He rolled over and threw up on the ground beside him. I retched all over again at the sight and smell of it.

When the heaving in my stomach stopped, I gulped pure, fresh air into my lungs. My knees were wobbly. I fell back against the gate and turned to climb it. My foot slipped on the bottom rail. I grabbed the top rail and I got a sure footing this time. I wanted to get away from Jason and the bull as quickly as I dared. They were both too unpredictable.

I clambered over, fell to the other side, and pushed myself dizzily to my feet. The fence was firmly between us, and on the other side of the gate Jason was a pathetic figure, lying in all that vomit. About thirty feet away, the bull stared at both of us, assessing the situation. Neither Jason nor I made any aggressive moves. After a few seconds, the bull snorted his disgust and turned back to the woods.

I ran the other way, stumbling across the field.

I moved by instinct. I climbed another fence, followed the next path into a little valley, then up over the next hill, needing to get to my favourite place in the world. It took forever, or maybe no time at all, to get to the cliff. There I collapsed on a rock. My heart was racing.

Caleb wasn't there. I was glad. I needed time to gather my thoughts. I was a little light-headed with nothing in my stomach. I looked down at the ocean. The sun was splintered into a million, blinding bits all the way to the horizon.

A noise behind me. I jumped up, startled.

It was just a harmless bird. A white gull taking off above the cliff.

If only I could spread wings and fly too. I closed my eyes. Amelia's face appeared in my mind. *Did some beam head ever grab you?* I asked her. Why had Jason grabbed me?

The answer came to me quickly. I'd laughed at him. Bullies didn't like to be ridiculed, and Jason had been a bully since we were little ones in the front row. Someone like Jason—and Jason's father—had to be treated like a mad bull: sidestepped if possible.

Suddenly, I knew I didn't want to see Caleb. Not this morning. I didn't want to blurt out anything about Jason. Something ached. I looked down at my hand. To my surprise it was still gripped tightly around the cedar rail.

I swung the piece of wood over my head, let it fly out into the air, watched it fall through sunlight and sky until it hit the water below with a white splash. It disappeared for a second only to bob up and settle on the waves and the ocean currents. Then I headed home.

CHAPTER 12

Right after my run-in with Jason, I collided with Dad at home. He was leaving for work.

"Whoa there, Meg. Where you rushing to?"

He reached out and caught me in his arms. He sniffed. "You sick?"

I looked down at my shirt. It was spotted with dried brown vomit.

"Yeah. No. I fell. I've got to change," I answered, unable to look Dad in the eye. I had to be careful. If I said one word about Jason coming after me, my dad would be on his way to the MacDonalds',

Uncle Art and Caleb with him. I wasn't sure I wanted that.

Will called out from the kitchen with a laugh, "Aren't you going to ask him to find you a pilot?"

Something shifted inside me. I yanked myself out of Dad's surprised hands. "How stupid do you all think I am? You treat me like a child. No pilot's going to take me up in a plane until this war is over."

I ran up to my room, close to tears. I slammed the door shut behind me and leaned against it. The truth of what I'd said met me in the mirror as I stared at my flushed face. Me and my crazy hope. The pilots in Sydney were too busy with the war to concern themselves with my small dream. Dad knew it; everyone knew it. They'd been humouring me like a little kid. Tucked into the wooden frame around the mirror, Amelia smiled at me from the frayed picture I'd kept there for seven years. I didn't smile back.

I ripped off the stinky shirt and threw it on the floor. On my dresser were two dimes. I put on a fresh shirt and shoved the money in a pocket. There would be a new movie playing at the theatre. Usually I'd take Will, but he'd laughed at me one time too many.

I watched out my window for Dad to disappear, then snuck out onto the back roof. One big jump and I was on my way alone to escape my misery at the Saturday matinee.

How Green Was My Valley was playing. It was a movie about Huw Morgan, a boy growing up in a small mining town in Wales. Just like me, he had to fight the bullies and earn their respect without the help of any older boys or his father. I sobbed my heart out feeling just like Huw Morgan. If only there were a Welsh prizefighter in Last Chance Bay to teach *me* boxing, I'd show Jason MacDonald what girls were made of!

I felt ready to face the world after that movie. Huw Morgan survived and so would I. My loneliness gone, I spent the evening in my room at home, preparing my speech. I wrote out a list of possible topics, things like: "What the Suffragettes Have Done for Me," "How to Handle a Bully," and "Beware the Rose's Prickly Thorns."

When I read the list over, I scrunched it up and threw it out. They sounded like titles for articles in a ladies' magazine. I knew in my gut what I had to speak about. There was only one thing I cared about *passionately*. The question was: would the whole town laugh at me if I went out on a limb and spoke from the heart?

On Sunday after church, I took my cousins to the beach. Caleb walked beside me. We walked in silence. I was debating how much to tell him. We sat on the rocks as the younger ones ran along the edge of the waves. The water was frigid, but Will and Stuart chased each other into it until they were soaked. Oblivious to the cold, they surfed onto shore pretending they were landing on the beaches of Normandy. Then they chased after the girls, pretending they were German soldiers and calling them "Huns." Sandra and Nancy screamed at them to stop.

Caleb broke the silence. "I waited for you at the cliff yesterday."

I was sorely tempted to tell him about Jason. I knew he'd give Jason a licking, which was exactly what Jason deserved. But then I remembered how Caleb was always caught in the line of fire between his parents at home. More importantly, this was my private war. I made a quick decision. I'd be like Huw Morgan. I wouldn't involve Caleb in my battle. Jason MacDonald was a problem I'd handle myself.

"I was sick." It was close to the truth.

"I missed you. I was hoping we could talk."

He seemed nervous about something, a little at a loss for words, but so was I. I'd never lied to

Caleb about anything in my life. The long awkward silence was back. I clenched my hands together almost as tight as my lips.

Caleb pushed his long bangs back from his forehead. He looked disappointed. "You getting headaches like Will?"

"Sort of."

"Did you pick a topic?"

"Amelia Earhart."

Caleb's expression changed. He threw back his head and laughed. "That's a grand idea, Meg. Grand. I was hoping you'd do that."

Just like that, the tension between us was gone. I didn't know why he was laughing, but I laughed too, knowing I'd made him happy.

"I don't know if, you know, if people will feel about her the way I do."

Caleb turned thoughtful. "That's exactly what Miss MacKinnon doesn't want you to worry about. You want people to understand the way *you* feel about her. Your passion."

"Oh, God, Caleb," I said, struck by a sudden insight. "Is this the suffering Miss MacKinnon talked about? How much I worry that no one will see her the way I do? That I'll look like a fool?"

"No. I think that's called Meg Christie's pride."

I whacked him on the shoulder. "Then I don't get the suffering bit. Thinking about flying makes me happy. Have you picked a topic?"

"Sort of." He turned away to stare at his brothers and sisters who were now digging up clams from the beach. "It's something to do with family and giving up things for them."

I could see only his profile as he talked. There was a scattering of freckles across his cheekbone.

"You mean sacrifice? Like your leaving school to work in the mine?"

He shifted uncomfortably. "I don't want to sound as if I'm full of myself. Everybody sacrifices things all the time. Look at our fathers. They both left school after grade six to work in the mines. Look at what soldiers do. Look at what our mothers do."

"I never thought of our mothers as suffering, although yours—" I stopped, not knowing how far I could go.

"My mother what?" His eyes were guarded, a sign I'd gone too far.

I reminded myself that we might be cousins, but we were not siblings. My dad had never laid a hand on my mother, and my mother didn't scream awful things at my dad the way Aunt Beth did.

"She's sick all the time," he said. His voice had a defensive tone that made me cautious.

"The tuberculosis," I said, but we both knew his parents had fought before his mom sat in the chair coughing.

"She should be in the sanatorium. She says we can't afford it. I think she's more worried about who'd take care of everybody if she weren't here."

I kept quiet. Aunt Beth didn't take care of them now. She rocked and worried and gave orders.

I was surprised at Caleb. He never talked about home. I knew things were hard for my cousins, but with Caleb spilling his guts, things had to be really bad.

"Didn't the doctor say she was contagious? Isn't she going to make everybody sick by staying?"

Both Caleb's hands shoved his bangs back nervously. I'd hit a nerve.

"It *is* better for everyone if she goes to the san, isn't it?" He stood up and began to pace in a little circle. He sounded as if he were arguing with someone. "I've been trying to convince her. So has my dad."

I knew Aunt Beth would explode if Uncle Art told her to leave her children. The arguments in his house must have been awful.

"I'm sorry, Caleb. Your parents sure don't seem happy."

"They aren't," he said tersely. "But they live the lives they do for us."

I'd overheard that line a thousand times at his house. *The only reason I stick around here is these kids. If it weren't for the kids, I'd be long gone.*

"Let's talk about something happier." He stopped in front of me and pulled me to my feet.

"I'm never getting married," I said.

"Good. You're too young and ornery." He smiled then and grabbed me around the waist.

I laughed, glad to forget problems we couldn't solve. He lifted me up and jostled me like a little kid. I didn't care. For three whole seconds, I was off the ground. My arms rested on Caleb's warm skin. I was in the circle of his arms.

"Mad Meg!" He cried, spinning me around. Three more heavenly seconds.

"You're bound for the sky, Meg Christie." He stopped and put me down. It was over. He took his arms away.

I shouldn't be liking him so much. I remembered the awful word.

"So if I talk about Amelia," I said, trying to hide

my guilt, "you'll talk about sacrificing your dream to help your family."

Caleb agreed. We'd both talk about the dream that kept us up at night. I could have written a tearjerker for Hollywood. If everything went according to my script, I'd be up in the air for the holiday and Caleb would be back on track, finishing the courses he needed for his high school diploma.

CHAPTER 13

Our public-speaking contest was bigger than Christmas, right up there with Easter and the Resurrection. You'd think the winner was going to win a million dollars or end up President of the United States. One thing for sure, the excitement wasn't caused by the leather-bound book Miss MacKinnon had promised us, although her collection included a copy of Amelia Earhart's *Last Flight* and I was keen to own it. Like the other contestants however, I had grand hopes of how the world beyond Last Chance Bay would want me *after* I won.

There were six students from the senior years, including Caleb and me, bent on winning. We knew darn well that an amazing load of good luck showered down upon the winner. The winner got this big helium balloon of success that lifted him—of course, it was always a him!—up and out of Last Chance Bay.

Maybe you have to know Last Chance Bay to understand. Last year Nate Ferguson won the contest. He spoke about journalism. In his speech, he pretended he was reporting from the front. Just before September, wouldn't you know it, he got a job for the Boston *Herald*. The year before that it was Alex MacLeod. Alex sang his speech. My mother had always said his voice was a gift from God. Alex sang solos for the miners' choir but after winning the Last Chance Bay public-speaking contest, he sang on stage in New York City.

My mom had insisted I try singing in the church choir but after a few rehearsals—I sing off-key—Mr. Robertson had a long talk with her, and the next thing I knew I was enrolled in tap-dancing lessons from Mrs. Cuthbertson. After the Christmas concert in which I shuffled through all the steps, knocking over the back row of tapping and kicking girls, Mom agreed that my gifts had nothing to do with music.

"How about flying lessons?" I'd suggested.

Mom frowned. "It's time you grew out of that, young lady."

Those words, *young lady,* had always been a rope around my neck. I was almost fourteen and she still strangled me with them.

"It's time you thought about more practical matters. I'm saving up for new curtains for your aunt Beth. There's some white cotton eyelet at the Hudson's store I've got my eye on. I need only a few yards and we could sew something pretty for her. Maybe I'll make a new dress for you, too."

I shook my head. Sewing curtains and dresses did not belong in the same breath as flying lessons. A leather flying jacket was practical for flying, not white eyelet.

My only hope of achieving my dream had resided in finding a sympathetic pilot at the airport. But since I'd faced how the war made that impossible, all I had left was the magic of the public-speaking contest.

Speeches had to be five minutes long. Five minutes was both an eternity and too short. Sunday evening I wrote out everything I knew about Amelia. At first it seemed impossible to fill three hundred spellbinding seconds. Then as I started rehearsing ideas and watching my clock, I quickly realized I'd run out of time before I'd reached the exciting bits.

Every evening I went straight to my room and worked on my speech. I had to win that contest. I *had* to. I presented it to Miss MacKinnon after school on the Wednesday before the contest, and her only suggestion was that I think about movies I'd seen and add a few gestures. "Dramatize it. Don't stand there woodenly," she said.

Before I knew it, we'd arrived at the last, glorious day of school. It was Friday, June 23. The sun poured through the windows into the schoolhouse, making my attention wander outside to the long playing field. It was a wide sea of green dotted with purple and yellow wildflowers bobbing under a blue sky. I was just starting to daydream that if I stood on my head maybe the sky could be the ocean, but then what would the flowers be growing down from the sky, when Miss MacKinnon said cheerfully, "Nothing like a clean window to help your dreams. *Videre* in Latin. To see. That's where we get vision from: both the things we see and the things we imagine."

Jason snorted beside me. I had only one more minute to endure beside that animal. Ever since I'd thrown up on him he'd been quiet around me, almost civilized. It seemed we'd both learned to give each other a wide berth. For my part, I ignored him and stayed out of his battle zone.

"Those of you speaking in the contest come up to the front of the class for a few moments. The rest of you are dismissed. I'll see you tonight."

As the class emptied, Jason, Savino, Bozana, Jane, and I moved forward to surround Miss MacKinnon. She stared out the window, that clean window, for a long time, then took a deep breath and fixed her gaze on Jason. Her voice had the sharp edges of an arrow flitting through the air toward its target.

"It seems that more than speeches will be judged tonight. Am I right, Jason?"

Jason's face turned red as a tomato. I guessed that Jason, or more likely Jason's father, wasn't willing to give Miss MacKinnon a wide berth. I wished I could tell her to try throwing up on them.

Miss MacKinnon turned her attention to the rest of us. "I want to wish you"—she stopped as if some emotion were stuck in her throat—"the best of luck. When you think about passion tonight, remember the poems I read you. If you speak with integrity about what you know is true, and if you go after it with all your heart, you'll pluck the purest chord of human experience."

I thought about Miss MacKinnon all the way home. She was the purest chord in all Last Chance Bay. In my room, putting the finishing touches to my speech, I rehearsed it to the mirror over my oak dresser. My speech was now four minutes and fifty-seven seconds exactly. I timed and practised a few dramatic looks, ones I'd borrowed from a new movie, *Since You Went Away,* until I was certain I'd beat out Shirley Temple if I auditioned in Hollywood. There was the "stricken" look with the back of my right hand thrown against my forehead (four seconds); "terror" with my eyes darting from side to side (two seconds, three different times during the speech); and finally "humble" with my hands clasped together and eyes heavenward (ranging from four to eight seconds). My plan was to end my speech with the humble, prayerful look. Its duration would depend on how long the applause lasted. I was praying for the longest standing ovation in the history of Last Chance Bay.

CHAPTER 14

The grass on the field behind the community centre was freshly cut for the end-of-school celebrations. The air smelled juicy green. Cuttings had been raked into a pile at one end, away from the stage and chairs, and the little kids dove into it and disappeared on top of one another like purple and yellow wildflowers. Joyful screams bounced across the field as parents and grandparents began to fill the chairs, calling urgently, "Get out of there. The speeches will start any minute."

I sat on a raised wooden stage with Jane, Bozana, Savino, Jason, Caleb, and Miss MacKinnon, waiting for the audience to settle. In the very last row I could see my parents and Will sitting with Uncle Art, Aunt Beth, and my cousins. They took up a whole row with Uncle Art safely pinned in the middle, his face the colour of home brew, unable to do anything embarrassing.

Jason's father, as the school trustee, stood barrel-chested and red-faced at the front of the stage with his arms outstretched as if Last Chance Bay were a seam of coal about to be split open by his pickaxe.

"Ladies and gentlemen. Boys and girls, order!"

A few skin-slapping smacks were heard as parents instructed their families to sit up and shut up.

"That's more like it. I now call upon Miss MacKinnon to introduce the public-speaking contest. Her students will show the benefits of a year under her tutelage. We'll soon be able to judge for ourselves what they've learned. Miss MacKinnon?"

There was scattered applause as Miss MacKinnon took centre stage. Something felt weird. I wanted to stand and whistle. What kind of introduction was that? Didn't Jason's father appreciate how many new ideas she'd brought us this year? How she'd asked us to look at everything with our thinking minds? How she'd given us our first year of enjoying school?

Sitting behind her as she stood to address the community, I saw something else that jarred. Her calm voice didn't match the clenched hands behind her back.

"I've asked the students to speak about something they feel passionate about and to start us off, Savino Calabrese."

A strain had crept into her voice. Watching her, I was reminded of times I felt cornered and had to explain my way out of an awkward situation.

There was nothing awkward, however, about Savino. "Marriage," he said dramatically.

Savino crossed himself, shook his head as if pondering this sacred subject, then crossed himself fearfully again. The adults tittered. I wondered if Miss MacKinnon had made the same suggestion to all of us: dramatize!

"Try to understand marriage from my point of view. It's terrifying. If you could see yourselves, you parents, the way we do, you'd be terrified too."

Savino was a natural comedian. Before I knew it, I was laughing at all the marriages in Last

Chance Bay, especially that of Savino's parents. His mother was a head taller than his father and weighed twice as much. She loved to argue with her tiny husband, even in public. But Saturday nights when she bent over and danced cheek to cheek with him she was a girl in love.

Savino ran through the plays of Shakespeare that dealt with the theme of marriage and ended up convincing us that marriage was the right and natural path for all human beings who dreamed of love. Unless you were a priest, like Father Michael in their Catholic Church, and devoted to God.

Or Meg Christie, I added silently, and devoted to flying. When the laughter died down, Jane Watson took Savino's place. I winced as she launched into her theme: writing letters to menfolk on the front was a critical part of the war effort. "Women have an important role to play," she said in her sweet, breathy voice. "We're changing the course of history."

Cripes! She sounded as if she believed women were responsible for D-Day! Keep the home fires burning, knit socks, and you too can push back the Third Reich. How could anyone in her right mind compare letter-writing and knitting with the terror of a battle, with being shot at and watching the corpses pile up around you?

When she finished, everyone opened their eyes and clapped. I sat on my hands as a protest.

Bozana Zawada was next. She'd spent most of her life in Jane's shadow. With her elfish face and short, auburn hair, even Bozana's looks made her far more interesting than pretty, predictable Jane. I was hoping for something unusual and she didn't disappoint me. She began her speech by humming a tune I'd heard many a Saturday night at the dances. Her face lit up and she swayed back and forth as if dancing a waltz. She stopped humming and asked if we could name the composer. It was none other than Frederic Chopin. I'd never heard of the guy. But Bozana claimed he was a famous musician from Poland. He'd written the most beautiful music in the whole world. He was so wonderful that the French claimed him to be a Frenchman. She spoke with so much passion I memorized his name and swore I'd listen for Chopin's music on the radio. At the end of her wonderful speech there was modest applause. I put my fingers in my mouth and whistled long and loud.

Jason swaggered to centre stage next.

"I guess it's fair to say Miss MacKinnon taught me *one* thing this year," he stressed *one* sarcastically. "She's forever asking us to look at the meaning of words."

Jason hadn't listened to one thing Miss MacKinnon said all year. And the last thing he cared about was the meaning of anything. Words? He'd never once opened a dictionary in ten years of coming to school.

"Let's take those suffragettes ... actually, somebody, *please*, take them."

There were a few undeserved guffaws among the audience.

"It's obvious why the word *suffer* is in their name because that's just what they'll do to the world if they take things any further. The world needs women to stay home and bring up their children."

Did the world need that from all of us? I looked at the back row. My mother smiled and waved at me. Aunt Beth had her eyes closed. Even from a distance I could see that her face sagged with pain and disappointment. Were they the mirror of my future?

"They insisted on the vote for women. What for?"

To my dismay, Jason had a good sense of timing.

"A good family votes together. In the Bible it says that women should obey their husbands. Seems to me the suffragettes were just a group of women no man would want to marry … not without a drink."

There were a few laughs. Who could laugh at Jason's crude jokes? I looked at the audience, furious.

Then Jason turned serious. I'd never seen Jason serious. "A woman's place is in the home. Why do women want to run for election? They have an important role to play. What would I do without my mother at home making dinner and running the house for us? I know it's thanks to my mother that I'm still in school and wanting to make something of myself. In return, it's up to men to be the leaders of countries, fight the wars, and do the hard work in the coal mine. Women …"

My mind went blank as the audience tolerated Jason's view of the division of labour. I was drowning in the ocean of Jason's words, dragged down by the force of his argument that would keep me in my place, unable to come up for air.

When Miss MacKinnon had taught us about

the suffragettes, I'd run home and asked my mother about them. "Weren't you glad when women got the vote?"

My own mother had sighed and rolled her eyes. "It makes no difference in the scheme of things. When I got married, I voted with your father anyway."

I scanned the faces of the women in the audience, mothers and grandmothers all of them. They might rule in the kitchen, but when it came to the affairs of the world, did they all obey their husbands? Didn't they have minds of their own? I looked at Miss MacKinnon and finally understood why she made my mother uncomfortable. There was no man beside her. She worked outside the home and spoke her own mind.

I was in big trouble if I didn't calm down. I couldn't be Mad Meg during my speech. I had to clear my mind and I was speaking in less than sixty seconds.

Amelia, I prayed silently.

No. I needed the big guns for this. *Mary Mother of God,* I prayed. *You were pregnant before you were married, shunned at the stable. It must have been hard for you. I need a little help here.*

Jason finished. People were clapping. I hoped it

was only out of politeness. My turn. Mary must have known I was going to have trouble and arranged our speaking order. Thankfully I was scheduled after Jason, not before. I had to be smart and use it to my advantage. I took a deep breath, ordered my knees not to wobble, and stepped to the front. I caught Miss MacKinnon's nod and began.

CHAPTER 15

"I had to sit beside Jason MacDonald all year. Believe me"—it was my turn for a dramatic pause—"Jason will do anything for a laugh."

Smiles went around the audience. I recognized friendly faces and smiled back at Sally MacEachern and her family, then Savino's parents.

Everyone knew Jason's reputation for getting suspended or expelled from school. He'd set the record for Last Chance Bay: fourteen times before he was nine. When his dad became trustee, that put an end to it.

"But on a more serious note, wasn't it grand that forty-five thousand women volunteers answered the Air Force and the Army and the Navy when they needed more help."

I swallowed my pride and gave my sweetest smile. If Jason could play the crowd, so could I. The cheering started and went on for a full thirty seconds. We were patriotic in Cape Breton and proud of our war effort. I made use of that half a minute to think. Now wasn't the right moment to add a wisecrack that women who signed up for duty earned less than men for the same work. I swallowed that comment the way I did cod liver oil in the morning: reluctantly. Everyone was cheering for women, wasn't that what counted?

I made a quick decision. I'd give the rest of my speech straight. The Shirley Temple act was out.

"Let me tell you about my hero. To me a hero is someone who does something that seems nearly impossible, when the odds are against you. My hero didn't grow up with much money, but wanted more than anything to learn to fly. My hero saved a small salary and whenever possible bought lessons to achieve that dream. Learning to fly before the war, before the Air Force needed pilots, wasn't an easy dream to achieve. And it was even harder …"

For some strange reason, I couldn't look at my parents.

"... for a girl. I'm sure you all remember the person I'm talking about. Amelia Earhart. She'd be flying missions over France right now, pushing the Germans back, if she could."

Their silence was wonderfully gratifying. They remembered her. Nodding heads assured me they remembered her spirit as I did. So I took them through Amelia's early years and biggest achievements, all the way to that fateful day, July 2, 1937.

"Sometimes I try to imagine what she felt as she looked out the window of her cockpit in those last minutes as she was going down. Here's what I see. A storm brewing in the clouds above, although below, the sun's still sparkling off the Pacific Ocean. The fuel gauge shows empty, and the motor sputters out. Suddenly it's very quiet except for the whistle of wind over wings. Waves look more and more defined as the plane drifts lower and lower. She can see the whitecaps now. They're getting larger. She feels butterflies of fear. Hundreds of them. And then she lets them go. Just like that, she releases them, and in their place she feels a strange sense of gratitude. This is the one thing she wanted to do all her life, and if she had to choose her hour of death, this would be it, doing what she loves best: flying."

There was a long round of applause. Amelia Earhart had come alive again, if only for five minutes. I beamed first at Miss MacKinnon, then at my parents. I turned and walked back to my chair. A suspicious little voice at the back of my head wondered if they'd be clapping like that if I'd come out to the very end of the limb and told them I was determined to fly one day too. But I didn't get to wonder long.

There was still one more contestant. The clapping died away, and Caleb rose from his chair and walked to the middle of the stage. He had a new brush cut. His ears stuck out, suddenly visible, and I found myself wondering if he'd sprouted wings.

Caleb took his hands from his pockets and began. "I've been wondering what I feel passionate about lately. When I was a boy, dreaming about what I wanted to be when I grew up, I thought, sure, I want to be a miner like my dad, like my uncle Norm. But then I learned about dinosaurs."

Caleb looked slightly embarrassed. "Don't take that the wrong way. I don't mean I wanted to be a dinosaur when I grew up."

Everybody laughed.

"I wanted to be an archaeologist and study the past. I know Miss MacKinnon thinks our coal comes from decomposing African jungles. That's the kind of thing I wish I could study."

There was an uncomfortable stirring in the audience. Some of the parents nudged each other, some lowered their heads to whisper. Caleb went on, oblivious.

"Most of you know I quit school when my dad broke his leg. Some days when I'm down in the mine working at the face I wonder if I'm as close as I'll ever get to my dream, that I'm digging up fossils of a kind. Down there you get a chance to look at things a little differently. It's funny being under the earth knowing your family is above you a mile up. In those hours I like to imagine how the earth was connected millions of years ago."

Some of the kids seemed restless, but Caleb pressed on. "Down there you feel how connected the earth is. It's strange to think what all the separation above the ocean has cost the world. The war in Europe could end if we won France back for the French. When I'm working in the mine, I imagine tunnelling under the ocean, coming up in somebody's backyard in Paris. It's unnaturally quiet because they're afraid of German soldiers. I imagine people staring from the windows, afraid to come out. It bothers me that there are no kids playing outside or a dad singing loudly on the back porch."

There were wry looks around the audience. Uncle Art's habits on his back porch were well known.

"In Europe families are staying inside, afraid of bombs and getting caught in a battle. So when I finish my shift and come back up to the earth's surface, I'm always surprised to see the sky and grass and kids and laundry flapping in the wind. Most days that eastern wind is our worst enemy, making everything dirty again."

There were smiles and nods from the women.

"But you know what? I feel happy, even when I see the dirty-laundry line. It's safe here."

Caleb looked embarrassed again. I bit my lip. A bomb was going off slowly, inside me. I knew what he was going to say next. How could he? Why hadn't he told me?

"This is my chance to say goodbye to everyone in Last Chance. I've enlisted. I'll be leaving tomorrow. I guess I feel passionate about what kind of world we live in and about getting to the end of this war."

There was a stunned silence. No one had seen it coming, but I should have. They didn't know Caleb the Rescuer as I did. Of all the nerve, enlisting! Without telling me? And what for? Someone else's backyard? What kind of dumb idealism was that? What about our backyard? What about his real dream? He was supposed to talk about helping his family while finding a way to finish school too.

My own cousin. With his five minutes of passion, Caleb pulled not only the rug out from under me but the sky on top of me.

Slowly the whole town stood up, clapping and whistling and banging their chairs for a standing ovation, the longest ovation in the history of Last Chance Bay.

CHAPTER 16

Forgiveness was overrated if you asked me. The judges picked Caleb as the winner. Miss MacKinnon presented him with a leather-bound copy of *The Odyssey*. I couldn't get near Caleb after the speeches. Everyone wanted to talk to him, big hero that he was. Jane threw her arms around him and planted a kiss on his lips. They looked as if they'd done it before. Lots.

It was a lovely June evening and the band started up in the covered bandstand. Most of the kids swarmed the dinner tables, loading up their plates with cold chicken, buns, and potato salad, then over to the dessert table to balance a slice of pie and cake on top of everything.

My stomach was in a knot. I stayed alone under a tree. Savino's parents led the first dance, cheek to cheek. Jane was stuck like a bloodsucker to Caleb, and next thing I knew, they were twirling around with the other couples.

That did it. Hot tears slid down my cheeks. I ran from the crowd to the other side of the community centre where a great round stump had been left like a stool for weary travellers. That's where I threw myself and cried and hiccupped, not knowing what hurt the most, my hopes, my pride, or my heart.

The moon was faint and low in the darkening sky. When my tears dribbled to nothing and my breathing returned to normal, I stared at the tall chimney stack rising over the trees. I knew it stood beside the mine. It pointed straight up at the sky as if trying to tell me something.

Was I a sore loser? A mean-spirited soul? A dreamer? A misfit in Last Chance Bay or maybe the entire world? I tortured myself, question after question, ready to cry again.

A twig snapped behind me. I jumped to my feet.

"Meg! What's wrong? I've been looking everywhere for you."

It was Caleb. Kissing Jane Watson? That's what he called looking? I gave him my best glare and prayed my cheeks were dry.

"You were supposed to be finding me a pilot," I yelled, letting my misery pour out. "Who said anything about you enlisting? What was so wrong with digging up dinosaur bones? I thought you were enrolling in correspondence courses. How come you didn't tell me? How come I had to hear your plans in the public-speaking contest?"

A whole pack of expressions swept over Caleb's face as I fired my questions at him. Confusion. Embarrassment. Pride. Hope. But there was one I hadn't expected. It caught me unawares. Even in the moonlight I knew the scar above his eyebrow was throbbing red.

He shoved his hands in his pockets. "You're upset about our dreams, is that it? You're different from me, Meg. You had Beryl Markham's plane come out of nowhere to give you your dream when you were six. It's like you got some direct line to God. It's not like that for the rest of us."

Caleb's voice made me feel I was supposed to feel ashamed. I didn't.

"My dad's leg gets broken and *wham!* so much for my dream. Every day for five months I've been working down in the mine. Life looks different down there. You can't imagine."

"You're right. I'm a girl. I'm not supposed to imagine or see the real thing. You're a boy and you can do it all for me. I'll never set foot in the mine to know what it's like, so you can tell me."

"Cripes, Meg. What makes you think it's so great to be a boy?"

"You have all the opportunities. Way more than me. And people respect you."

"Opportunities. Right. I'll go fight in the war rather than go back to school." That look again. "The thing's done." His voice was tight. "I'm sorry I didn't tell you. After I'd done it, the contest was the only way to tell everyone. It's complicated, Meg."

It didn't make a lick of sense. I was feeling ugly and crabish. I wanted to pinch and hurt with my red claws.

"Well, anyone can give up on a dream."

His mouth dropped open. "You wouldn't."

"Is that what it takes to get the whole town behind you?"

"I didn't enlist to get the town's approval."

"Then what was all that crap about fighting for our backyards?"

Caleb went pale as a bleached sheet. "Remind me not to fight for yours."

"Don't you remember that poem we learned last December? There is no honour dying in war, just a lot of blood, and men dying."

"I'm so glad we're having this farewell."

I was on a roll. He wasn't going to leave so easily. Maybe I could get him to un-enlist. Was it possible? I'd memorized the last lines of the poem and I preached them at Caleb now.

"'My friend, you would not tell with such high zest to children ardent for some desperate glory, the old lie: *Dulce et decorum est / Pro patria mori*.'"

Caleb lost patience. "Spare me. We all had to memorize those lines for Miss MacKinnon. Men aren't stupid you know. I'm not going for some desperate glory or patriotism. And in case *you* don't remember, Miss MacKinnon nearly got fired for teaching that poem with a war going on."

"She should have taught more. You didn't get the message."

"Don't you know what Hitler's doing to people over there? It's a different war, different reasons.

And now, after D-Day, we're so close to the possibility of ending it."

I wasn't saying what I really wanted to say. I didn't even know what it was. I kicked the tree stump.

"I'm mad at you, Caleb. You were supposed to help me with my dream, not change yours. I'm not going to give up *ever*. And I wish … I wish …" My words were stuck. I was holding myself tightly.

Caleb smiled suddenly, a puppy smile that caught me off guard. "You wish I weren't going? And that we should never give up? We should never forget our dreams?"

"What is this? A movie?" I whispered.

I hadn't asked him my burning question yet, and it was smoking a hole in my tongue. "When did you enlist anyway?"

"I was going to talk to you about it, but it was that Saturday when you got sick. I got a ride into Sydney and ended up at the airport. By the way, I *did* ask around if there might be a pilot to take you up."

"And?" A crazy flicker of hope.

"Sorry, Meg. It's not going to happen now. All the pilots are involved in training there. As soon as the war's over, you'll get your chance."

I wasn't surprised. It was the answer I'd steeled myself to expect. But I was on a roll with self-pity and not about to stop. All too clearly I remembered that Saturday again. What miserable, rotten, crappy luck. What a pair of secrets we had kept from each other.

Bad luck was still stepping on my heels. From around the corner of the community centre, Jane Watson appeared in the moonlight.

"Am I interrupting something?"

"Yes," Caleb said.

"Yes," I said, a second behind him. But in the next breath, I felt overwhelmed all over again by what he'd done, by where he was going. I started backing away, barely avoiding the tree stump. "No ... just forget about me. I'm getting a headache. I'm going home. Congratulations."

"Come over in the morning?" Caleb said quickly. "Come say goodbye."

I was only his younger cousin, but I wanted to give him something to toss and turn about. Something to wreck any possible plans to dance the night away with Jane Watson. I turned to leave with a nonchalant toss of my hair.

"Maybe."

CHAPTER 17

When he's drunk, Uncle Art complains that women are too emotional, always in a snit about something. I say thank God for women's emotions. But I hated being in a snit with Caleb, and what a tangled snit it was.

I was the one who tossed and turned all night, waking at dawn to the sleepless conclusion that I would go and give Caleb a send-off, a Meg Christie send-off, whatever that might be. At least he wouldn't forget me.

It didn't take long to get to his house. Already the sun was busy lighting up the sky, but it wasn't going to reach inside me—not until I'd had my say. Caleb was just leaving the privy when I cut through the houses into the back of his garden.

"You still going?" I called out. It wasn't what I meant to say, but the real words, the words of saying goodbye to Caleb, were buried in bedrock within me.

Calmly Caleb threaded the end of his leather belt under the loops of his trousers, then looked up at me. He was dressed in his best funeral suit, a hand-me-down from his father that didn't flap around him any more as it had last year.

"You still mad at me?"

What a question! Would I always be Mad Meg to him?

I kicked at one of the wooden cages holding new tomato plants. Just then, Charlie tore out from the back of the house. The whack of the screen door made me stop kicking. Charlie rushed past us toward the privy.

"Look out!" he yelled.

Stuart charged out next, cussing worse than a miner, hot on Charlie's heels. He banged on the privy door that Charlie had locked on the inside.

"I'll kill you."

We could hear Charlie's voice through the door. "No, you won't. I'm never coming out."

"You got no business in the privy. You peed it all in the bed again."

We heard sniffles.

Caleb walked over to Stuart and pulled him back toward the house. "Calm down. You can have my bed while I'm away." He pushed Stuart up the steps.

"Why can't that little moron do his business in the privy. You hear me, Charlie?"

The back door slammed as Stuart stormed into the house.

There were more sniffles from the privy. Caleb walked toward it and knocked on the door.

"Not coming out."

"Stuart's gone."

"He's going to tie me up in the stinky sheet and throw me in the ocean."

"No, he's not. He's going to eat breakfast. He's going to forget all about it. He's going to sleep in my bed while I'm away and you won't have to share one. Now get out of there before you fall in."

"He says I do it on purpose. He says I make him a miser."

"Not miser, Charlie. Miserable. He says you were born to make him miserable. But don't believe it. Stuart comes by his misery naturally. He used to wet his bed too."

The latch scraped across the wood from inside. The door to the privy squeaked open and Charlie poked his head out, checking to make sure the coast was clear.

"He did? God's truth?"

"He did. We all did. You'll grow out of it soon. Don't drink tea at night—makes it worse. Let's go eat. My ride'll be here soon."

Caleb whacked Charlie on the head. It was some kind of male signal.

Somehow, while I watched Caleb coax Charlie out of the privy, my anger drifted away like one of those dark clouds you tell yourself to keep an eye on, but after you've been distracted, you look up and find it's gone.

"You coming, Meg?"

I straightened the homemade cage surrounding a newly planted tomato plant, a scraggly little green thing. My parents loved gardening. They said the tomatoes would grow and burst through the cage if we had a good summer. There wasn't much else to do but follow my cousins up the little path through the garden to the back of the house and into the kitchen.

Beside the cast-iron stove, Aunt Beth sat in her rocking chair. The bottom of her face was hidden by a cotton rag, but I could see her eyes. They were glazed over. She nodded at me, speechless from a coughing fit. Her rag was blotched with red stains. How long before someone else got sick?

Aunt Beth's blanket had fallen behind her on the floor. I picked it up and tucked it around the bones of her shoulders.

"Oh, Caleb," her voice broke. "I try to save you from one thing, and there's another lurking around the corner. If only your father—"

"Aw, Ma. Don't start on that. I'll be home before there's snow on the ground. The Allies will win back Paris and then we'll force Berlin to surrender. Think of the Christmas we'll have together."

Aunt Beth looked more miserable than I'd ever seen her. Caleb knelt beside her and took her hand while he spoke softly.

"Remember what we promised each other?"

Aunt Beth shook her head.

"Yes, you do, Ma. I didn't join the Air Force because you asked me not to. You thought a miner would be safer on the ground than in the air. So now you must keep yours. I want to know only one thing while I'm overseas: that you're getting better in the san. My army pay is good. It'll cover it, I told you that."

"But you'll need money for yourself."

Caleb laughed and squeezed her hand. "I'm going to be fighting in a war, not sightseeing. I don't need it, Ma. You do. And Sandra's almost twelve. That's plenty old enough to take care of things around here for a few months. You're not helping anybody sick."

Ah ha! So that was it. Caleb was defending home in more ways than one. He'd found the way to make Aunt Beth promise to go to the sanatorium. Lordy, these men. I couldn't help think it wasn't exactly fair. He'd go off to war, and Sandra, as the eldest, could grow up quick and help run the house. On the other hand, Sandra and all my cousins were doomed to catch tuberculosis if Aunt Beth didn't leave.

I finally understood what he'd done. And because of my foolish pride, I now had only one precious hour before he left Last Chance Bay. It was time to stop sulking.

"Right. We girls can manage the home front," I said. "My mom and I will help out too."

Aunt Beth waved her hand at the ceiling as if there were a bees' nest overhead. Uncle Art.

If I could take care of Jason MacDonald, Uncle Art was nothing. I rolled up my sleeves.

"Caleb, you go up and see about clean straw for Charlie's mattress and I'll make oatmeal."

There was nothing like work to get my mind away from useless thinking. In no time everyone, including Uncle Art, was crowded around the kitchen table for a Last Chance version of the Last Breakfast. For once, Uncle Art and Aunt Beth didn't bicker. There was some muttering between Charlie and Stuart but not enough to upset the table.

Caleb sat on my left, our elbows brushing. Caleb's hand kept going up and down from his bowl to his mouth. My eyes were drawn to his right hand. I memorized his long fingers. He kept his nails trimmed square and neat. Several times he stopped and poured enough maple syrup into his bowl to sweeten a cranberry bog.

I put my spoon down, stood up, and poured the kettle of hot water into the sink to start dishes. There'd be bedding to wash upstairs, so I filled the kettle and set it to heat again.

Caleb's ride honked outside. I looked at the clock. Less than an hour! I'd been cheated. I filed outside behind my cousins. Caleb hugged everyone. When it was my turn, I held onto him as long as I dared, then looked into his eyes. They were the colour of the sand on the beach where we'd played every summer.

"Goodbye, Caleb. I'll miss you."

For a second—what a second—I thought he was going to kiss me, on the lips, right there in front of my cousins. I was ready to forgive him everything. He could change dreams like he changed shirts, I didn't care. Caleb's sweet breath sang across my skin, up and down every artery and vein, along every nerve of me.

He smacked his lips against my forehead. A proper cousin's kiss. These were his parting words to me, God's truth:

"I won't expect socks, kiddo."

CHAPTER 18

The school committee, led by the school trustee, fired Miss MacKinnon the day after the public-speaking contest. They accused her of "inappropriate teaching goals." They said she was inciting her students to irrational acts of passion and no good would ever come of that.

Up until now I hadn't understood why passion made a person suffer. I was beginning to understand it now, how it crept up on you, a surprise attack, just before it swallowed your heart whole. Miss MacKinnon had stood up for what she believed in, and Last Chance Bay was going to make her suffer.

"Can't you do anything?" I screamed at my parents.

"It's too late," my dad tried to calm me down. "Angus MacDonald told her they didn't like her style of teaching. He said she could stay until the end of July if she had no place to go. She told him she didn't, but didn't intend to stay one day longer where she wasn't wanted. She'd take the next train to Halifax. That means tomorrow, Meg."

They looked at me sheepishly. "It's water under the bridge," my father added. "I'm sorry."

That's what Dad always said for a situation that was over and, in his books, best forgotten. But I wasn't prepared to forget.

I'd barely survived saying goodbye to Caleb. After Caleb left, I went to sit on the cliff overlooking the sea. I sat with my knees bunched up tight against my chest, locked under my arms, rocking myself, needing comfort. The gulls kept calling unintelligible things to me, calling and playing on the wind currents. I asked them to fly across the ocean and watch over Caleb.

The very next day I had to say goodbye to Miss MacKinnon at the train station. My parents brought Will and me. As we approached her on the platform, I was sure Miss MacKinnon wiped something from her eye. My parents shook her hand, the way adults did, and said they were sorry she was leaving. All polite, looking at the ground, the way adults did. My mother said she was sure, or should she say hopeful, that Miss MacKinnon, with all her education, a fine thing, a good thing, would find another job in Halifax quickly. She stammered as she failed to find the right words, but I knew my mother was trying for my sake.

Will was tongue-tied. He shook hands and kept his eyes on the ground.

Then my dad said they'd wait for me outside the station. I was left alone with Miss MacKinnon.

A wall of suitcases surrounded her like a shield. She held herself stiffly, as if she'd been thrown from a horse.

My farewell with Caleb had taught me one thing. I only had now. I wasn't going to stare at the ground. I went right to the point.

"I want to apologize for all of Last Chance Bay," I said, my voice trembling with anger and sadness. "It's not right. You were the best teacher we ever had."

"Some of the parents didn't think so."

"Who? Mr. MacDonald. This is his doing. And Jason's. Those two wouldn't know a diamond from a lump of coal."

I'd penetrated the shield. The old teacher look returned to her eyes and a little smile lifted her mouth. I was about to be corrected. A porter picked up Miss MacKinnon's bags and we talked as we followed him, side by side, to the last car.

"I believe you're wrong about that, Meg. Truth reveals itself in different ways to different people." Her arms relaxed and she became thoughtful. "For you and me, the freedom to discuss new ideas is a diamond. Who knows? Give them more time, more pressure, and maybe the MacDonalds will see a diamond there too."

The porter climbed the iron steps leading into the last car. Steam billowed between us. Miss MacKinnon reached into her handbag and handed me a leather-bound book.

"In my mind, you and Caleb were tied for first place. You deserve a prize for your speech."

"*Last Flight*," I whispered, reading its cover, "by Amelia Earhart."

I stood there as tongue-tied as Will had been, unable to thank her. I'd burst into tears if I tried to say what I was feeling.

"First Caleb … now you …" I was losing it.

She put her arms around me and gave me a long, warm hug.

"You'll have your first flight, Meg Christie. And when you do, I want to hear about it. Write to me and I'll write back."

I loved her dearly, but I didn't believe her. The chances of my getting up in a plane were as likely as Miss MacKinnon staying in Last Chance Bay.

She boarded the last car and after a few seconds, I saw her again through a window, settling into her seat. Her eyes found mine and she waved, a sad smile on her face, her fingers wiping her cheeks quickly. We watched each other as the train lurched into movement and pulled out of the station. I knew she could see me for a lot longer than I could her. All too quickly the windows and then the train itself became a blur, then a dot, then nothing.

I didn't go outside to meet my parents and Will, not until the train had been gone for a long time, disappearing into the point where the tracks met. The book, Miss MacKinnon's gift, felt hot and heavy in my hands. It was wonderful of Miss MacKinnon to give it to me. I'd treasure it. But the truth was I'd lost too much. The speech. Caleb. Now Miss MacKinnon.

Amelia Earhart would never fly again. Amelia Earhart was dead, just as Will and Stuart had always insisted. The truth was I'd never learn to fly. I would never get out of Last Chance Bay. Like the train, my dream had vanished from my horizon. Life was as rock bottom as it could possibly get.

What did I know about the future and dreams? Outside, my brother Will took one look at my face and tried to cheer me up with his favourite dumb saying.

"Things could always be—"

I did what boys would do to shut him up. I whacked him.

Little did I know. Will was right. Things were about to get worse.

CHAPTER 19

"Why can't I go?" I begged. "Will's been down in the mine lots of times. I've never been once."

It was mid-August and the day before the miners' holiday. The whole town was abuzz with vacation plans, even Jane Watson, whose family hardly had two dimes to rub together, was boasting about their plans to visit Boston. Not us. Ever since my dream of flying had taken a lengthy vacation, a dark mood had hovered over me. Week after week the sun shone, but I never smiled. I banged the door when I came home. I slammed it when I left. There was nothing to look forward to.

It was the worst summer of my life and I couldn't even look forward to school starting in a few weeks. Who would they get for a teacher? I was stuck, stuck to a life and a place I'd never chosen. Whenever my mother asked me what was wrong, I exploded at her. "Why couldn't you send me away with Miss MacKinnon?"

There was something else too, something I couldn't talk about. A strange ache had started in my chest the day Caleb left. Savino's father had lost a hand in a mining accident and called it his ghost hand. I called the dull ache my ghost Caleb.

Caleb had written us every week from his training base. He didn't say much, just that training was intensive and tough. They were desperate for more men overseas in what would hopefully be the last offensive: driving the Germans to surrender in Berlin. Every letter said the same thing: he was exhausted in the evening and missed us. Working in the mine had prepared him well since there were aspects of training he didn't like, but just like in the mine, he did what was asked anyway. Going to war would be a long shift in the hardest pit of all. At the beginning of August we got his last letter. They were as ready as they were going to get. They were going overseas soon. He was nervous but glad the waiting was over.

There was only one thing I enjoyed all summer. It was reading *Last Flight*. Reading that book, I knew that as Amelia's fuel ran out and the dark ocean loomed close outside her cockpit, she *had* felt the strange gladness to die flying that I'd imagined during my speech.

Since Aunt Beth left for the sanatorium, I spent my days with my cousins, although the ache in my chest got worse over there. I usually did the laundry outside while my mom and Sandra scrubbed and cooked inside. Caleb's clothes were noticeably missing from the line of socks and shirts.

Then in August, a few days before the holiday, while pegging Charlie's sheets to the line, *Last Flight* gave me the idea for an unexpected kind of adventure. Amelia Earhart had explored the world above ground; I'd go below. I'd be the first girl in Last Chance Bay to go down in a mine. The thought of seeing Pilot again made me smile.

Dad's eyes loomed white out of his coal-dusted face as I cornered him in the front hall after work. "The mine's no place for a girl. That's a fool notion, Meg."

Strangely, Mom stepped out of the kitchen to take my side, her hands covered with pastry dough, her voice sympathetic. "She's good with animals, you've said so yourself. Couldn't you at least try to get permission? Surely they'd let her help bring the ponies out for the holiday?"

"What's got into you two? No girls is no girls. You cause any trouble and they'll be giving me a permanent holiday."

I had to find Will when it was time for supper. He was down at the Calabreses' trying to beg junk from their shed to build a tree fort.

"It's not fair," I argued with him all the way home. "You'll have plenty more times. You already went down a few days with Dad this summer. Let me take your place."

"You wouldn't like it. There's rats down there." He made chomping noises with his teeth, right in my face.

Boys! I wanted to smack him.

But then, after dinner, I noticed Will kneading his fingers into his temples. Mom and Dad were visiting neighbours, and we listened to a show on the radio before going upstairs. He was fighting one of his headaches. It was an omen.

"You're getting sick," I said, fighting to keep the excitement out of my voice. "You won't be going anywhere tomorrow." Meg-of-no-mercy, I trailed him into his room.

Eyes dull with pain, Will curled up on his bed.

"No girls," he moaned, waving me away. "Dad'd kill us both if you're caught. That's only if the foreman doesn't get you first."

"Everybody says we look like twins," I argued. "I'll wear your big coat and cap and no one will know the difference. I won't speak to anyone—oh, please, Will, please."

"When Dad gets home, tell him I'm getting a bad one," Will moaned again.

Sounded like a yes to me.

When my parents came in, I went down to the kitchen where they were talking. They stopped and watched as I grabbed a few carrots from the vegetable bin.

"You hungry?"

"Yup. Good night."

I hadn't been friendly for weeks, so tonight wasn't anything special. Walking slowly up the stairs, the quiet murmur of my parents' voices wafted up from the kitchen again, something about Miss MacKinnon, Caleb, the holiday.

Hmmpf. If they felt any concern, it was too late.

In my room I pulled on pants, wrapped myself in my blanket, and tiptoed back into Will's room. He was sound asleep. I lay on the other side of his bed, on the floor out of sight, under his window.

Will would be fine in a couple of days. I reminded myself of the opportunities he'd have. He could work in the mine alongside Dad next summer, or in a few years swagger off to Europe if the war didn't end. Or maybe he'd surprise us and go down to the docks in Sydney or Halifax and find work on a boat. He'd send home postcards from Europe or India or South America, places I'd only traced on a world map at school.

That night as I was going to sleep, my chest didn't ache as much. Wherever Caleb was, he was doing what he'd thought best. I had an adventure ahead of me. It wasn't my dream, but I was almost happy for the first time that summer. I fell asleep thinking of Mr. McArthur's barn and the gentle little pony with the mark across his back. Would Pilot have changed? Would he remember me?

The next thing I knew, my father's time-to-go knock on Will's door startled me awake. Will groaned and rolled over. Half-asleep, I stood up, stumbled across the room, grabbed my brother's coat, shoved my hair under Will's cap, and ran downstairs. By the door, Dad stood with two metal lunch pails ready for us and yawned sleepily, eyes shut. I rushed outside past him, my heart racing. So far, so good.

CHAPTER 20

The morning of my adventure, the sky looked like a giant seam of coal, trapped between night and morning. For the first time in my life, I joined the eerie shadows of men walking to the colliery. Dad didn't talk and I was thankful. The men grunted hello, or nodded silently, then fell into step, half-asleep, I guessed. The ocean made its presence felt as a smell—a strong, kelpy smell—and I shivered with excitement. Soon I'd be hundreds of feet below all that water, meeting Pilot.

Then at the lamp house, the entrance to the mine, the man in the booth with a bald head like a third eye stared at me hard.

"This your son?" he asked.

I froze.

Dad stood behind me. He thumped my back and laughed. "Who else would it be?"

Nervously, I glanced back at the man, but he was nodding, not concerned about me, already looking at the next miner. My fingers shaking, I took the proffered lamp, clipped it to my cap, and ran behind Dad to climb into the rake. What a relief when it jerked to life. The train began its long, rattling descent down the sloping rails into the dark deep where I'd be well hidden.

Over the squealing of the wheels, I heard our neighbour, Hector O'Connor, tease my dad, "I guess Pilot will be flying out o' here tonight."

Dad smiled at me. "That's why I brought Will here. Will has a firm hand. He'll keep him calm."

I nodded mutely. He'd be Dad-of-no-mercy if I didn't keep quiet. The train jostled and jerked, almost rocking me back to sleep. I wasn't paying attention and nearly missed the moment when it slowed to stop. Dad jumped off with the other drivers and I scrambled after him. If I were Will, I'd probably know where to go, what to do. I had to stay alert, not give myself away. I smelled horses. We were at the underground stable.

Before us squatted a long wooden building, built into the rock. My lamplight moved above the dark stalls searching for Pilot's name. Dad was ahead of me, already opening a stall door, leading a sturdy pony toward me. In the shadows it was hard to tell if it was Pilot. His wide-set, unblinking eyes looked right at me.

"Hold him for me," Dad said. "I'll attach the shave."

I moved forward to hold him. "Hello, Pilot," I whispered into his twitching ear.

The pony snorted. Did he remember me? I reached out both hands to stroke his long neck. Close up, I saw again he was grey. My hand moved down his back. There, across his rump, was the strange black island—Pangaea.

Pilot turned his head and nudged me hard in the side.

Did he know I'd packed carrots in my pocket? If these ponies were smart enough to keep a miner from danger, they were smart enough to smell treats.

"Think I've brought you something?" I asked.

I held one out in my open palm for him. I felt the strange kiss of Pilot's fleshy lips as he took the crunchy root from me, nudging me again.

"He's thanking you," Dad said, eyeing us as he attached the wooden shave that joined Pilot to an empty cart. A sharp *cling* of a metal pin announced it was time to work. Pilot's ears straightened and I knew it was time to join my father behind the cart.

Without a word, we headed into the tunnel. I'd heard enough stories to know our job. We'd go from room to room, loading the miners' coal into the cart, then we'd haul it through the dark maze of tunnels to the landing where it would be taken to the surface and weighed.

"Just for a minute, turn off your light," my dad said suddenly. "Keep your hands on the cart."

I couldn't help myself; I gasped. We were in total darkness. It was just as Caleb had tried to describe to me. The darkness dominated everything. For a moment, it snuffed out all my senses. Then gradually, I thought I could taste its coolness. I could smell its ancientness. I could feel our closeness to the centre of the earth. I imagined that I could reach out and touch the darkness like a solid thing.

I began to feel something for which I had no name. Was this akin to what Amelia had felt—this fear mixed with wonder? Human beings did not belong here: this was not our world. My fingers touched something solid. It was the edge of the coal cart. I gripped it tightly and heard a new sound: my father's breathing beside me. Then another sound entered my awareness, a harsh, steady rhythm. *Clop, clop. Clop, clop*. I recognized it with surprise. It was the sound of Pilot's iron shoes on the rocky floor. Pilot kept moving, oblivious to the dark.

"How does he know where to go?" I whispered.

"That's a fool question," Dad answered sharply. "Pit ponies do. They can guide you out of any situation; that's why I'd trust him with my life." He switched on his lamp and then mine.

Light! Hungrily, I moved my head, shining the light over everything: my father's large hands beside my smaller ones, Pilot's tail flicking from side to side, the chiselled walls of the tunnel and the timbered ceiling overhead.

As the first hours passed, my muscles began to ache, but my spirits stayed high. We worked steadily, loading the cart with coal, trudging behind Pilot through the tunnels. This was my adventure.

Jane Watson would come back with stories about shopping in Boston. What would she say if I told her I had worked in the mine with the men?

As our shovels scraped into the coal, my father sang in his deep bass "The White Cliffs of Dover." I barely stopped myself from joining in. If Dad found me out, he'd do more than call this a fool notion, and I was no fool.

My hands were getting blistered. I was glad when Dad said we could stop to have lunch with Hector O'Connor and his buddy. We opened our lunch pails just as the safety examiner arrived to check the room for gas.

"The machine's not working," he announced. "I had to bring the—"

The look on my face stopped him. The examiner held out a long stick. At the end, a tiny bird stood trapped in a tiny cage. This was another story I'd heard many times: how the bird would die if there were a dangerous leak of methane. Poor thing. I couldn't bear to watch. I stared down at my sandwich. My fingertips left long, dark shadows on my mother's white bread.

My father leaned over and spoke to me quietly. "We use a machine now. But before it was invented, it was the bird, and before the bird, it was a man holding the flame on that stick, praying for no explosion."

I looked up at Dad. He had a queer look in his eyes as he continued. "Hector and Art are going to dynamite open a new seam. I'll stay and help them. You take Pilot and the cart up to the landing. Someone will be there to help you unload it."

Alone?

He felt my fear. "Just follow Pilot," Dad said. His owl eyes stared at me calmly. "Remember to trust him. Always trust your pit pony."

Right then and there, I nearly confessed, *it's me, Meg.* But I remembered what he'd said about my fool notions, and how Will had laughed at me, saying the mine was no place for a girl. I thought about Caleb off in the war. I thought about Miss MacKinnon leaving on the train. And finally I thought about Amelia. People had told her the sky was no place for a woman; she never gave up. Was I a complete coward?

Keep your mouth shut. I told myself. *It's the one thing you must do today.*

All too quickly the cheerful sound of my father laughing with the men disappeared behind me. I was alone in the dark underworld, following Pilot. The air was damp and musky.

Clop, clop. Clop, clop. I held onto the sound of Pilot's clopping like a rope.

Suddenly, in that tunnel under the bedrock, under the ocean, Pilot stopped.

I heard scurrying. There were rats ahead of me, behind me, everywhere.

"Move, Pilot," I croaked. My desire for adventure was disappearing, shrinking to the size of a bird in a cage.

Pilot snorted and shook his head.

What was wrong with him? Was I to be trapped here forever? Eaten by rats? First—and last—girl in the mine?

I lurched forward. My headlamp flickered over the coal inside the cart, then Pilot's sweaty flank, then the dark hole. I clung to Pilot's hot, damp neck and made myself stare into the tunnel. At first I saw only the dark hole, then my lamplight illuminated something on the floor, blocking our way.

Relief filled me. I collapsed against Pilot, laughing. "It's just a fall of rock. Just a stupid bit of rock."

There was a shovel on the side of the cart. I used it to clear away the rubble, singing "The White Cliffs of Dover" as loud as I could. In no time Pilot would lead me through the tunnels and up to the rail where someone would unload the coal for me.

Light shone around the corner in the tunnel ahead, and I stopped singing, hoping they hadn't heard me.

Pilot led the way and we turned the corner. Lamps hung from the support timbers around the rail line, and under the angles of their lights I saw something that made the hair on the back of my neck stand up, something worse than a giant rat. I was alone in the mine with Jason MacDonald.

CHAPTER 21

My heart pounded so loudly in my chest I was sure Jason could hear it. I tried, but I couldn't make Pilot back up. I was stuck.

"Hey, Will," Jason sang out. "That's a fine load you got there. Let me help you with it."

I nodded mutely and moved up to stand by Pilot's head as if trying to calm my pit pony. If there was one person who'd delight in ruining my one day of freedom, it was Jason MacDonald. If he found out it was a girl—not any girl either but me, Meg Christie—under my brother's hat and coat there'd be a price to pay to keep him quiet.

I studied Jason carefully. His face was streaked with sweat and coal dust. He moved quickly, intent upon his work, humming cheerfully. He unloaded the cart onto the track. He didn't seem the same Jason who slouched in his school desk and bullied us in the schoolyard, or the Jason who'd grabbed me. Down here he sang and worked hard, one of the men.

"Turn your pony around, Will, and I'll attach the empty cart," he ordered.

I did as I was told, happy to move away from him.

"There. You're all set, Will," he said, walking around to clap me on the shoulder. From another tunnel we heard the clopping of another pony and saw flickering lights that meant another cart was approaching the landing.

"Best be on your way now, Will. It's going to be crowded here in a minute, like a traffic jam in a big city." He laughed at his own joke.

I nodded, smiling stiffly, afraid to say anything and give myself away. Jason stared at me, stared at me real hard and quizzical.

"No time to stand around talking about girls, Jason MacDonald," the miner with the new load called. "Get over here and do your job."

The awkward moment passed and I hurried away. I welcomed those black tunnels with a huge sense of relief. I could only hope I didn't have to meet Jason again that day.

The way back was uneventful. By the time I reached Dad, they had opened the seam and I forgot all about Jason MacDonald.

At quitting time, we walked by Wilhelm Kraus's underground garden. Under the glow of bare light bulbs Pilot stopped and lowered his nose to smell geraniums.

Then my dad bent beside Pilot and did the same thing!

I was so surprised a laugh burst out before I could stop it.

Dad laughed too. "It's a habit. We do this every day, don't we, Pilot?" Dad said, rubbing Pilot's nose gently. "You'll be smelling a lot more than a few geraniums very soon now."

I thought about that image all the way back to the stable, Dad leaning over to smell a few flowers in the dark mine, something I'd never seen him do in my mother's garden. The drivers removed the ponies' shaves and piled them outside the closed-up stable. Everybody was laughing and joking.

"I won't have to smell Angus's onion sandwiches for a whole week!"

"I'm going to sit and listen to the radio all day and the company's going to pay me!"

Sensing something was different, Pilot whinnied a question over and over: *why wasn't he returning to his stall?*

"It's a holiday," I whispered. "You're going up, out of the mine. It's going to be so wonderful. My brother and I will visit you every day, seven whole days outside."

"Blindfold him," Dad said. "He's not seen the light of day for a while, remember. It might blind him completely, if he's not already."

Gently, I placed my coat over Pilot's face and tied the sleeves behind his ears. The little horse stamped one hoof and tossed his head.

"Trust me," I said over and over, until finally Pilot stood still. Then we joined the other drivers and horses walking up the two-mile slope.

We neared the surface, and the darkness started to change, as if layers were being pulled away. It lightened to dimness, and then shadows, and then, in a blaze, we were out. Light exploded around us. I closed my eyes and nuzzled close to Pilot, who sidestepped uneasily. When I opened my eyes again, the first thing I saw was my father's blackened hand, holding Pilot's bit.

We led the horses to a large, open field. Dad told me to run ahead, and I obeyed, opening and closing the gate after the ponies were all inside. I could hear the soft, deep voices of the men speaking to their horses, crooning. Then they removed the blindfolds and backed away slowly toward the fence, climbing atop the worn, wooden rails. I climbed up, too, and I sensed my father passing me Will's coat, wrapping it around my shoulders. I was spellbound, caught up in watching Pilot. At that moment I *was* our little horse.

At first all the horses stood still, shocked by the breeze rustling their manes, the fresh air filling their lungs, and the smells of growing things. The light assaulted their eyes. Light was everywhere, so, so bright.

They shook their heads and blinked ... it was still there ... all that light.

Pilot was the first horse to move—only a few steps at first. Then he seemed to know he was free and he bolted. The others followed, flying across the green field, kicking up their heels, wild and abandoned.

One by one, the miners rose, clapping and cheering. When I felt my father stand beside me, I stood too. The men tossed their caps high in the air. I went to toss mine too, but my father clamped his hand firmly on my cap, fixing it to my head. I turned to look at him. Suddenly, I remembered my long hair. My girl's hair.

The briefest of smiles cracked across Dad's coal-dusted face before he removed his hand.

Dad knew. I'd gone down in the mine, all day, and he knew. Beside him, now, something small inside me expanded until I felt as tall as the sky. I kept my hat on and waved my brother's coat wildly, cheering loudly with the other miners, watching the horses tear across the field.

We were the last to head home. Dad didn't say one word. I wondered if he felt the way I did. I'd broken all the rules going down and I'd survived! My feet didn't touch the ground. I'd spent a whole day working with the men down in the mine, a wonderful day. No one could ever take it away from me.

There were purple wildflowers, lupines, clustered in the deep, green grass at my feet. I picked seven, one for each day of the coming holiday. When I sniffed them, I saw again my dad leaning over the geraniums in Wilhelm Kraus's garden. I remembered the sounds I'd heard that day, the steady scrape of shovels, the men singing, the scurrying of rats, and the *clop, clop* of iron shoes turned to pounding, the wild drumming of horses' hooves suddenly free in a green field—Pilot's first flight.

At home, Mom stared at us, speechless. She looked from me to my dad. "Will's sick. He's been asleep all day. I thought *you*"—she looked questioningly at me—"were over with your cousins."

Dad nodded and placed his hand on my head again. "There's more under this hat than meets the eye. And it better stay quiet about what happened today."

I nodded, realizing there'd be no telling Jane Watson. There'd be no telling anyone. My breath caught in my throat as I realized there *was* one person I could tell, the best person in the world. I'd write Caleb and tell him. He'd keep the secret. I'd knit him socks, too—now *that* would make him laugh!

I passed my mom the flowers and kissed her on the cheek.

My mother grabbed me and gave me a warm hug before she pulled away and laughed. "Bless me, if my prayers haven't been answered. Now, have we heard the last of the slamming doors for a while?"

CHAPTER 22

The morning before the holiday ended, a man knocked at my cousins' door. I'd started knitting the socks for Caleb, but since I didn't know how to make the heel, Mom was going to show me later that afternoon. The knitting needles with their balls of grey wool sat on the table beside the door. My mother had offered to hang up the mountain of laundry if I'd finish up in the kitchen, then get the little ones out of her hair. She was out back, singing as she pegged. My cousins had gone ahead of me to the beach.

A cold tingling started in my chest when I heard that knocking at the door. No one from Last Chance Bay knocked at your door. They just walked in.

I put the last clean dish to dry in the rack and hurried to the door. I passed my pile of knitting and wished I'd started those socks a lot earlier, back in July.

"This the Wisharts' place?" the man outside said. He wore a blue uniform and stood as stiff as a tree, holding a little envelope.

All I could do was stare. Immediately, I knew why he'd come. Maybe I suspected with the tingling, but I knew for sure staring at that envelope. It was a telegram and I'd heard about them.

"Mr. Wishart home?"

I shook my head. Uncle Art and my dad had gone fishing.

"Mrs. Wishart?"

I shook my head. Aunt Beth was miles away in the sanatorium. If I didn't answer maybe he'd leave.

The man stared down at the envelope, then back at me.

"You related to Caleb Wishart?"

I was wanting to say no, wanting him to be at the wrong house. Swallowing hard, I nodded.

"I have a telegram," he said. "I'm sorry. I usually read it out loud. Do you want to sit down?"

I stood there, blocking the door. I didn't want him to read it. I wanted him to go away and never come back. But I couldn't speak. I was fighting a crazy impulse to slam the door in his face and finish the socks for Caleb. If I finished the socks, maybe this wouldn't be happening.

He opened the envelope and read the telegram. The words jabbed into me, sharp little jabs, without normal punctuation to ease the message into everyday meaning.

"'Deeply regret to inform you 81698 Private Caleb Wishart reported killed in action sixteen August 1944.'"

Caleb was a number? An image of Caleb filled the room: Caleb leaning against his bike, squinting at the sun, laughing.

The man handed me the telegram. "Do you want me to sit with you? Are you alone?"

I shook my head. I didn't want him in the house.

"Go away," I said, as politely as possible. I closed the door and walked blindly out through the kitchen to the backyard.

"Mama," I cried, holding out the telegram. I hadn't called her Mama for years.

Bad news was in my voice, on my face. She looked at me sharply, took in the telegram, and dropped the sheets. Clothes pegs fell from her mouth and hands as she ran to me. She took the paper from my outstretched hand and read it. She read it twice and then a third time, not wanting to believe it.

"Oh, no," she cried. "Say it isn't so."

She looked at me. Something broke in her, the same thing that was breaking in me. We held onto each other and sank to the back steps.

At times like that, I knew I was lucky to have a mama, my mama. She rocked me in her arms and we cried for a long time. Having her so close kept the ghost Caleb away, but when our crying time was over and I had to stand alone, it was back with a vengeance. I felt as if a bomb had gone off in front of me and ripped off my chest. It wasn't the mine that got him. It wasn't the tuberculosis. It was the war.

CHAPTER 23

Dear Miss MacKinnon,

I wish I were writing to tell you I had my first flight in an airplane, but I haven't. I don't have good news, although I wonder if you've heard already.

Caleb is dead. He was killed in his first days of action while fighting to liberate France. I miss him. Everybody does. I know that you of all people will understand how we feel.

I'm writing you because of something else.

Last week, the miners had their first paid holiday, a whole week. We didn't go anywhere and at first I was disappointed. Now I'm glad, for it meant that we were at home with my cousins when we got the news about Caleb. It wouldn't have been right to be anywhere else.

I'm also glad we stayed home because I spent the whole week with Pangaea, my dad's pit pony. Dad let me change his name from Pilot to Pangaea. It was my first choice for his name, after all that you taught me about the world.

Did you know that the miners made sure the ponies got a holiday too? Pangaea had a wonderful week, until the end. After the telegram came about Caleb, I went to talk with him. Animals are the best friends. He listened to me and he understood all that I was feeling. I understood him too. He's loyal to my father but it's dark and lonely down in the mine. It's a terrible place, and I know Pangaea dreaded going back after his week running around a green field.

I can't disclose how I know so much about what it's like in the mine, but trust me, I know first-hand. They call it the pit because that's what it is. Maybe because it's so awful, the miners are careful to treat each other really well, and that includes their ponies.

The end of the holiday itself was a terrible day. My brother and some of the boys in town had to help the miners get the ponies back down into the mines.

The ponies knew what was coming. They kicked up an awful fuss, whinnying like crazy, tearing around the field. They were desperate to stay free. I haven't seen Will cry for years, but he cried fighting with Pangaea. There was no other way. It took hours. Everyone was exhausted. Two men were injured by the time it was all over.

Are you sitting down? Something happened to Jason MacDonald. I can't say too much, just that we got to talking after they got the ponies back in the pit. Jason and I fell to talking about this and that, and then he said, "Miss MacKinnon was the best teacher Last Chance Bay ever had."

God's truth, he said that. One thing led to another and yesterday, a few days after the miners went back to work, my dad came home looking at me strangely. "Angus MacDonald phoned Miss MacKinnon asking if she'd come back, if she hasn't found a job. She said she hadn't found a job yet. Without a good reference from Last Chance Bay, it was impossible to get another posting. She didn't think she'd want to come back here, but he asked her to think about it. He said 'she's too strong-minded for my taste in a woman, but what the hell, I'm not married to her.'" (I'm sorry to write that, but those were Mr. MacDonald's exact words.)

So I'm writing you to say you were right. Last Chance Bay can tell the difference between a diamond and a lump of coal. I don't suppose Mr. MacDonald said it like this, but we need you. If you don't come back, we don't want to go back to school. Please reconsider.

Sincerely,
Meg Christie

I sent that letter off even though I felt as if I was begging. Here in Last Chance Bay we like to hold our heads high. *Never ask for charity. Neither a borrower nor a lender be. You made your bed, now lie in it.* But this was not the time for Meg Christie—or Last Chance Bay—pride.

When Will found out I'd written a letter, he sat down and wrote his own with Stuart and Charlie. They all signed it. "She can't think it's just the girls who want her back," Will said proudly.

I was so impressed with him, my migraine little brother, I didn't know what to say. I nearly hugged him, but just in the nick of time I remembered to whack him on the head, the male signal of happiness.

"Thanks, Will."

There'd been rumblings all summer from the parents who'd liked Miss MacKinnon and rumblings, a certain August afternoon, from someone unexpected.

I suppose, technically, I lied in that letter, making it sound as if Jason MacDonald had a change of heart and thought Miss MacKinnon was our best teacher. I hoped God would understand and forgive me. But if Miss MacKinnon came back, she'd never need to know any different because Jason MacDonald would be working in the mine, not stirring up trouble in her classroom.

Besides, since there were certain things I'd promised to keep under my hat, I couldn't very well repeat to Miss MacKinnon everything that happened, everything that was said, there in the field where the pit ponies enjoyed their holiday while the sun painted the sky all orange and purple above the hills behind us.

That last afternoon of the holiday, Dad and Will were having a heck of a time catching Pangaea. Since the telegram arrived, we'd all been in a mood to scare off the devil. The holiday had ended prematurely for us with its arrival. When the trainers approached the horses in the open field carrying their ropes and bridles, Pangaea, like all the other pit ponies, sensed that this was his last moment under the open sky. He kicked and bucked anyone who came close, including my dad, whinnying a furious refusal to go back to the mine.

Jason MacDonald lassoed him from the fence and then my dad yelled, "Get those ropes over his neck. Hold him down."

I stood on the fence, staying out of the bedlam. I knew the men would yell at me if I interfered or cried out.

When they had several ropes around Pangaea and he finally stopped bucking, I jumped off the fence and walked up behind Will. I couldn't sit on the sidelines. I had a big carrot in my pocket and I snapped it in two, holding the pieces on my palm. My dad glared at me. I'd never seen him in such a mood. Steam could have billowed from his mouth and nose he was so foul-tempered by the whole affair.

I held out the orange root offerings on one palm and wrapped my other arm around Pangaea's neck. Fear poured from his sweaty hide onto my skin.

"I know what you're afraid of," I whispered in his ear. "That dark place. I don't blame you one bit. I wouldn't want to go back there either."

I hugged him tight, forcing my eyes to stay dry. "You've got to go, Pangaea. There's no other way. But you'll be free one day. You just have to keep hoping you'll be free."

A shudder passed through his body into mine, followed by an angry resignation. He shook his head one last time to let us know his opinion, but I sensed his resistance was over.

I heard my dad say in a grim voice, "Blindfold him now."

I watched Dad and Will lead Pangaea into the mine. I knew it would be the last time I'd see him. Once again, I'd betrayed him. I didn't like the choice, but I accepted it.

Jason stood in the field some distance from where I sat brooding on the fence. I was wondering what Caleb's last few seconds had been like. I didn't know. I'd never know.

I stared at Jason, his back to me, looking off in the direction the pit ponies were led away blindfolded and subdued. When Jason turned around to face me, there was a strange look on his face. He had something on his mind. He walked slowly toward me, head down. I sensed he didn't mean any harm, but wanted to talk about something. I remembered the day in June that he'd grabbed me. I nearly jumped off the fence to run home, but I didn't. I might as well hear what he was coming to say.

I kept my arms crossed over my chest. I didn't trust Jason MacDonald any closer than I could hit him with a fence post.

He stopped a few feet away. We were in each other's battle zones.

"Sorry about Caleb ..." he said, his voice trailing off.

I remembered that he and Caleb were the same age. They'd grown up together. Maybe they were friends. I didn't care. I wasn't about to discuss Caleb with Jason.

I nodded curtly.

"You got a special way with that pony."

"Guess so." What on earth did he want?

"It was a lousy way to end the holiday."

"Guess so."

"The ponies won't get a holiday next year."

I felt as if he'd slapped me. "That's not fair."

"No," he said. "But neither was this. It was hard on everybody, them too. It felt terrible to do that to them. Big Mick dislocated his shoulder and Fergus MacLeod won't be seeing out of his right eye for a week. He nearly had his brains kicked out. I'm not looking forward to Monday morning."

Jason looked a bit like a fish gulping for air. "It must be awful to get a taste of freedom, and then lose it. I never imagined they'd kick up such a fuss."

It was all I could do *not* to make a comment about the state of his imagination.

"That was a crazy thing you did last week."

What did he mean? It was my turn to gulp air.

"Aw, don't look like that. I knew it was you, not Will, in the mine."

Jumping Judas! Jason was going to get my dad into a deep pool of trouble. My hands turned into fists. I didn't have a weapon, but I was prepared to fight, lie, whatever it took.

"You're wrong. Ask Will. It was him, not me."

He gave me a Jason MacDonald look, full of malice. "You don't think much of me, do you, Meg Christie?"

My silence answered him better than any words.

"Guess I got it coming. Letting that bull out like I did last June. Grabbing you."

What was he saying? The words didn't say *I'm sorry* but the voice and face almost did. I shook my head much the way Pangaea shook his.

"My dad or Mr. McArthur would've killed me if you'd told, so"—he straightened his shoulders—

"I owe you. For a girl, you got brains, Meg Christie."

The urge to annoy him was enormous. "I didn't know you appreciated brains."

"You mean because of Miss MacKinnon?"

That and a million other things. The list against him was long, but Miss MacKinnon was at the top. I nodded.

Suddenly Jason laughed. It was more of a smirk. Bully Jason was back. "I'm going to keep working in the mine. I'm not going back to school. My dad said he can't find anyone to teach you. He might have to rehire Mr. Panzorire. Remember him?"

"He wouldn't!" Who could forget Pants-On-Fire? He'd kept a leather switch tied to his belt. One day he got so mad at us, he had a fit and backed into the stove. I almost smiled, remembering his scorched pants and how he couldn't sit down for three weeks.

Jason looked as if he'd played the worst prank in the world. "He would! Miss MacKinnon had too many new ideas. Mr. Panzorire lives for only one idea: beating the crap out of his students."

I narrowed my eyes at Jason MacDonald. It was easy to imagine the bull's head. I could feel my blood boiling, but I remembered to be cautious. Maybe I could divert his attention.

"If Mr. Panzorire comes back," I said, "I may not go back to school either. Maybe nobody will. All the boys will work in the mine."

"That'd be stupid." It was obvious he didn't like the idea.

"No. Getting Miss MacKinnon fired was stupid."

"It's hard to talk to you, Meg Christie."

"So don't talk."

I hadn't done very well at controlling my temper. We glared at each other for a while. The sun had set and everything was in shadows. I could smell the strong kelpy smell of the ocean, not far away. Suddenly I was aware of the ghost Caleb. He was standing between me and Jason. *Come on, Meg,* he urged me. *Get on with it. Use your brains.*

I took a deep breath. Did a bull have pride? Could I appeal to Jason's now? "You have influence, Jason. We'd all look up to you if you made your dad ask Miss MacKinnon to come back."

Jason hooted. "He'd do that only if I threatened to enlist."

"Why's that?"

"My dad fought in the Great War. It's gruesome

when he talks about it, especially about the mustard gas and the wounded men. He doesn't want me fighting. He likes me working in the mine. He hopes with my education I'll be manager one day."

For a second, the smirk left Jason's face. He looked strong and proud again like the young man I'd glimpsed unloading coal from a cart. If he couldn't be decent above ground, why didn't he stay down in the pit where he belonged?

"You said you owed me," I said. "We'd be even if you could get your dad to phone Miss MacKinnon."

Jason seemed to consider this. It took him a very long minute to think it over, probably because of the rust in his brains, but to my surprise he finally said, "For what it's worth, Caleb once told me Miss MacKinnon was the best teacher we'd ever had. I'll do it for Caleb. I'll see what I can do."

Jason stared at me hard. He hated me and I hated him. It was one of those things that was never going to change. But I could feel ghost Caleb standing there between us, putting the pressure on.

I kept my mouth shut.

Jason continued, "You just make sure you tell Jane Watson and all the other kids the right story: that it was my doing."

Jason tipped his cap at me and swaggered away.

Would wonders never cease? I turned and walked home. I felt as if I'd made a deal with the devil, but that night, two nights after we got the news about Caleb and the night after the pit ponies were forced back into the mine, Jason MacDonald must have gone home and blackmailed his father into asking Miss MacKinnon back.

To me, he was every bit as loathsome as he'd always been, but he'd given me plenty to think about. Even if he was motivated to impress Jane Watson, even if he did it to pay his final respects to Caleb, he was planning to do something that might turn into a small Last Chance Bay miracle.

It seemed time that I, Meg Christie, revised my thinking. Maybe the boys in Last Chance Bay weren't such a bad lot after all. My brother, Will, and my cousins, Stuart and Charlie, might be lumps of coal but there was hope for them. They might turn out like Caleb and become diamonds.

Still, walking home that night alone, breathing in the last smells of summer, I was glad to be a girl.

CHAPTER 24

September came. I turned fourteen. I woke up remembering the wish I'd had for the longest time. It felt strange. I didn't want to be a boy any more.

I went to sit on my stage, the cliff overlooking the Atlantic Ocean. The earth was full of mystery. A supercontinent did exist millions of years ago. Powerful forces had divided Pangaea. Even if I was the only one in all of Last Chance Bay to believe such a thing, I *felt* those forces—they acted on us still. They'd acted on me. We were changing every minute of every day, in the mine or above ground, though it was slow and invisible to our eyes.

After two full months in the sanatorium, Aunt Beth's health had improved. She wasn't well enough yet, but we were hopeful she'd be home before winter. We were grateful her health had improved by the time the bad news came about Caleb, or she wouldn't have survived at all.

Every morning, except the morning I went into the mine, I made breakfast for my cousins. I got everyone tidied up and fed before my mother arrived. With Aunt Beth gone, it was easier to get things done. Her rocking chair, where she'd sat coughing, stayed quiet by the stove. My mother imposed her health and order freely in her sister's absence. Monday was washing day, Tuesday was baking, Wednesday she sat at the Singer sewing machine, and so on through the week. For my mother, every day had its own domestic purpose. I no longer saw it as woman's work. My father could have done it, or Will, just as my mother could have worked in the mine. I knew this now, just as I knew my place was in neither of their worlds. I'd find my own way, just as Caleb had tried to find his.

My mother knew better than to keep me indoors all day. I went out with the boys, chopping wood and bringing water, fetching this and that, and then I was in charge of taking all of them out of my mother's way when she needed us out of the house.

Inevitably we ended up on the cliff overlooking the beach. Our stage.

"Meg, come quick. Caleb's been shot down and we need an ambulance driver."

They'd been drawn to this subject like moths to a light the last few weeks. Caleb had been blown up, operated on, amputated, awarded the silver cross, lost in action, or sent home on a stretcher, all variations of the same theme, on our outdoor stage.

The ghost Caleb was hurting too much; I lost patience with them.

"Not Caleb," I turned around and hollered at them. "Can't you play something else?"

Little Charlie ran over to me, blinking like crazy. His blinking had gotten worse. It was exhausting to watch his face.

"It was Stuart's idea. I told him I don't want to play any more."

"Come here, Charlie. Come talk to me." I pulled him onto my lap and wrapped my arms around him. His warm, small body filled the wounded place outside my chest, dulling the pain.

"Do you miss him?"

Charlie nodded.

"Me too."

"He was supposed to come back. He promised."

"It's the war. It wasn't his fault."

We were quiet, watching the waves way out with their white slippery tongues.

"Your mom will be home before Christmas. She's getting better. And you know who else is coming back?"

His wiry body tensed with excitement. "Miss MacKinnon?"

"She'll be here next week. That's why we're not in school yet. We're waiting for her. She changed her mind. We weren't the only ones to write. The Calabreses wrote. The MacEacherns. Even the Watsons. My dad wrote her too and promised he'd run as the new school trustee. See? Miracles do happen. People do come back."

His whole body smiled. I could feel his hopefulness. Blink, blink, blink.

I pushed him to his feet, then myself. "I should get back and help my mom."

He offered me his hand. "I'm coming with you. I don't want to play with Stuart."

We were halfway back to his house when we heard the drone.

"Look, Meg. What's that?"

I followed his pointing finger into the sky. A plane was getting closer and larger. The quiet drone became a roar as it flew directly overhead. It was an old biplane with bright red wings and an open cockpit.

"Hmm. That's funny. I haven't seen one of those since …" I remembered the last time I'd seen a Gypsy Moth. It was years ago. I didn't think the Air Force owned any now.

"I used to tell Caleb I was going to fly one of those."

"Why?"

"It's a long story. I've wanted to fly since the day Caleb and I watched Beryl Markham land in a bog."

"Don't you want to any more?"

I watched the plane bank, dip its wings, and head away, back toward the ocean.

I sighed, starting to walk again. "Sure I do, Charlie. I keep hoping it's going to happen one of these days."

Charlie's house was already in sight when I heard Will yelling behind me.

"Meg, come back! Meg!"

Charlie and I turned to wait for my brother.

Will caught up with us, grabbed my hand, and yanked me into motion. "You've got to come."

What now? My mind started racing along with my feet as I followed my brother back toward the cliff.

"Who is it? Who's hurt?"

But Will let go of my hand and was running full speed ahead of us. I couldn't keep up, not while holding onto Charlie. To my surprise Will didn't head up to our stage at the top of the cliff but took the path that led down to the beach. Someone must have gone over. My stomach lurched. I looked to my right to the bottom of the cliff but I could see nothing but white spray above the grey rocks. It wasn't until we were halfway down the path that I looked straight ahead to the long flat beach. There I saw something that made me realize we weren't racing to pick up the dead body of one of my cousins.

On the beach was our reason for running. The tide was out, exposing a mile-long, forty-foot-wide, hard, damp beach. It was a perfect landing strip for an airplane. The red Gypsy Moth rested there, and beside it my other cousins were talking to the pilot.

"He must be in trouble," I said, helping Charlie leap over a rock on the path.

"What if it's a German?" Charlie said fearfully.

In front of us, Will had stopped to wait where the path met the beach. We caught up and walked together.

Will whistled in amazement. "Can you believe it? We're playing air battles, and a plane comes out of nowhere and lands on our beach."

"Maybe it's the Red Baron," Charlie said.

"That was in the Great War," I said, laughing. "They don't have dogfights in this war."

Will was bursting with excitement. "He asked for you, Meg. The pilot asked if any of us knew a Meg Christie. That has to be you, right?"

I laughed in disbelief. "Asked for me? Come on, Will. You expect me to believe that?"

Will grabbed my hand and forced us to run the last twenty yards. "He did. He did. Ask him yourself."

My cousins moved aside to let me stand, panting like a thirsty dog, face to face with the pilot. He wore an RCAF uniform. I relaxed at the welcome sight of his blue suit. He wasn't a German.

"Meg Christie?" he said, removing pilot's cap and goggles.

Will wasn't making it up. My mouth dropped open and I stared from Will to the pilot. I nodded, looking into clear blue eyes. The pilot stared back at me. I watched the black moustache wiggle with a shock of recognition.

"Billy Buzz?" I gasped.

"Captain William Hughes." He laughed. "Billy hasn't buzzed since before the war."

I was struck dumb.

Will poked me in the side, trying to poke me back to my senses. It was useless. I was stuck in the memory of Billy Buzz and a thunderstorm at the Sydney airport in 1939 when those red wings had last disappeared from my life.

Will asked defensively, "What do you want with my sister?"

Again Captain Hughes wiggled his moustache. His words made no sense to me. Like someone speaking under water, they were all garbled.

"I'm here recruiting and training. I happened to meet a Caleb Wishart in England before"—he paused, noticing how we flinched at the mention of Caleb's name—"before he was killed. I'm sorry. He was a terrific lad. When you're from Cape Breton, far from home, you find each other. We got to talking in a pub one night. I told him the story of meeting a young girl from Last Chance Bay just before the war, a girl who wanted to fly more than anything in the world. He laughed and said that could only be his cousin, Meg Christie."

I gulped. There were no words in my head or my mouth. I was stunned. The world was reeling. Caleb talking to Billy Buzz?

Will, however, had no trouble speaking. "I know all about you. You promised her a flight and you never gave her one."

The friendly mood changed. My cousins eyed him warily.

Captain Hughes nodded, putting his hands out protectively. "And I'm here to apologize. Don't look at me like that. You all look so much like that young man Caleb. I promised him I'd look her up when I got back. See? Here I am. I'm keeping both promises."

The thought of Caleb talking about me, thinking about me, so far away, made a hundred Gypsy Moths take off in my stomach. The ghost Caleb became Caleb flesh if only for the seconds I imagined him alive as he was a month ago, talking to this man.

Once again Will did the speaking. "How were you meaning to apologize?"

A smile lit Captain Hugh's face. He held out a set of goggles to me. "Want to fly?"

"Yes," I croaked. My voice leapt from my throat. "Yes!" I snatched the goggles, before he could change his mind or disappear in a lightning bolt.

He held out his hands to boost me up onto the wing. There were two tiny seats in the cockpit, one behind the other. I knew to climb in the front one. I slipped into the seat, smelling leather and oil.

Captain Hughes swung himself up onto the wing and leaned over me with a few instructions before he slipped into the seat behind me.

"That's the control in front of you. If you make a mistake, I can correct it, so don't worry. If you want to head her higher, just pull the control toward you. To go down, push it gently away. Left and right, the same thing. Small movements. Okay?"

I nodded, too excited to talk. I was about to go up in a plane.

"See that tube?"

He pointed to a black hose that ran along the side of the cockpit from his seat to mine.

"We'll talk to each other through that. It's too noisy otherwise."

I'm sure my cousins cheered as we took off, but the drone of the motor was the only sound in the cockpit. My stomach took off too when the nose of the plane suddenly lifted and the ground moved away.

I was in the air.

We kept rising. Ahead of me, all around me, there was only open sky. We banked to the left, over the land. Below me, I saw my cousins jumping up and down, getting smaller, smaller, quickly shrinking as if they'd taken a magic potion. Ha! I laughed. My brother, Will, was the size of a toy! So was the chimneystack and the mine and all the houses of Last Chance Bay.

The land stretched below us for miles and miles. I saw not just one hill, but a flock of hills stretching out from town into the interior. They were spotted-looking, feathered with different shades of green. The nose of the plane lowered slightly, and we began to fly at a level height, no longer rising. Billy Buzz banked steeply, this time to the right.

We were heading out to sea. I hooted with joy! Below us the cliff was a brown step rising above the white waves of the bay. I could see that it was only a small part of the whole landscape, the edge of the mass of land that was Cape Breton. The shoreline was a cliff rising from the Atlantic, worn smooth over time and from the battering of the wind and sea. From this height, the strangest transformation was in the trees. What were tall trees when I stood beside them had become tiny, green stubbles from the air.

My mouth hung open with the wonder of it. Is that what the world looked like? So big! Below us, everywhere, there were waves in constant motion. The ocean was a mysterious-looking place with currents that went both ways: they could take you out, but bring you back home too. Above the ocean, the sky went on and on, one sky above one continuous earth. Just as Caleb had imagined, I could see beyond Last Chance Bay. We were all connected. *Videre,* I thought, remembering my Latin. I can finally see.

From the little tube beside me, I heard Billy Buzz's voice.

I picked it up and put it to my ear. "How are you doing?"

I spoke into it. "Great!"

"We could arrange … few lessons … Sydney … Sunday afternoons."

"Okay," I shouted. I couldn't hear every word but I got the gist of what he was saying. I had no idea how I'd do it. But I'd do it. I'd get there. Even if I had to do without movies on Saturday, I'd get there.

"Want to fly her now?"

I looked down at the Atlantic. *No, don't look down.* It was Amelia speaking to me, on my right shoulder. *Keep your sights on the sky.* It was Caleb with me, on my left.

"Yes!"

I knew exactly where I wanted to go. Ever so slightly, I pulled the control toward me. I felt the immediate response of the Gypsy Moth. What a thrill. She was under my hand, obeying.

This was where I belonged. I'd arrived. My smile stretched as wide as the sea and I flew that Gypsy Moth up into the open sky.